Choosing You
The Cedarville Series #3
by
Bree Kraemer

Choosing You

The Cedarville Series
Bree Kraemer
Published by Bree Kraemer, 2020.

Choosing You

Also by Bree Kraemer
The Only Series
Only By His Touch
Only With Trust
If Only
Only You
Only For Love
Cedarville Series
An Unexpected Home
Capturing Us
Choosing You
Better Together
A Chance Worth Taking
Forever Starts Here (Novella)
After All These Years
Won't Let You Down
Say When
Something to Lose
Finally Home
Friends & Brothers
Sky High Love
Bridge To Love
When It's Love
Rockstar Romance
The Right Note
Pick Me
Christmas Novella
Light Me Up
DecorHATE for the Holidays
Falling Over You
The Beckmeyer Family
Hooked
Sparked

Shocked
Kneaded
Valley Falls Strikers
Late Tackle
First Touch
Give & Go
Narrowing the Angle
He's A Keeper
Ground Rule
Walk Off
Sacrifice Bunt
Grand Slam (coming soon)

Chapter 1

The saying went, when life handed you lemons, you make lemonade. But what were you supposed to do when your lemons were brown and rotten?

You throw them in the trash and drown your problems in vodka. At least that was what Carly was doing. And who needed a glass; it tasted better straight from the bottle.

Practically slamming the bottle on the table, she laid her head down and closed her eyes. The house was quiet except for the low snoring of her dog, Max, from somewhere in the living room. Only months ago, there had been people around all the time. But, now that both Leah and Mel lived with her cousins, Brandon and Logan, Carly was alone.

And fuck that, 'just because you're alone doesn't mean you are lonely shit.' She was lonely. And sad.

Lifting her head, she took another drink from the bottle of vodka. At twenty-eight she knew better than to try and drink her problems away, but when she'd come home from the studio, alone, it was the only thing she could think to do.

Sure she could go out to a bar or restaurant and meet up with other friends but her heart and head just weren't into it. She missed her friends, and for one night, she was going to let herself wallow in self-pity.

Taking the bottle, she stood up and walked to her couch. She loved her life in Cedarville, wouldn't have changed it for anything. But sometimes, it was hard to be the odd man out. And technically, she wasn't, not really. Together, she, Leah and Mel ran Dragonfly Dance. Meaning six days a week she spent hours upon hours with her two best friends. And more times than not, they went out after work for dinner or drinks and the guys joined. But it wasn't the same.

Before, she'd had someone to bitch to at all hours of the day, but now, if she wanted to talk when she was home alone she had to text or call.

And honestly, that was just too much work for her.

Flipping on the TV, she changed channels until finally settling on some dumb reality show. She figured if she watched these crazy people for just a little while, her life and problems might not seem so bad.

She had barely been watching for two minutes when her phone rang. Glancing at the screen she saw it was a blocked number and she declined the call. Five months ago, the calls had started. She had to hand it to the guy, he was persistent. Five months of daily phone calls and the same message over and over.

"Miss, Graham, this is Samuel Bruce. I'm calling on behalf of your mother. If you could please return my call at your earliest convenience, I would appreciate it."

She'd stopped listening about two months ago. Instead she'd delete the messages and move on with her life. She had no idea if the messages had changed in that time and didn't really care. She wanted nothing at all to do with her mom. Seven years ago, she'd made her decision and she still stood by it.

When you found out your mom was a whore who'd cheated on your dad your whole life, and then you caught her sleeping with your own boyfriend...It was not a hard decision to cut her out of your life.

The memory of walking into her boyfriend's room and finding him in bed with her mom still haunted her. She didn't think it would ever go away. That day shaped her life and not for the best. It was the reason she wasn't willing to unlock her heart. She swore no man would ever have the power to break her again.

And that only added to her loneliness. Yes, she could have sex if she chose to, but when you lived in a small town, you had to pick who you slept with wisely. Otherwise you would end up with a guy who wanted a relationship.

And that led to the other reason she was lonely. Lack of sex when everyone around her was getting some was problematic. A vibrator could only do so much. Orgasms were fine and dandy, but when a girl wanted comfort and a shoulder to lean on, they fell short.

She sighed and tried to clear her mind of the image that popped up. Damn him for interrupting her wallowing.

Anthony Scott.

Even thinking about him pissed her off.

But it was hard to stay angry with him when there was no reason to be angry in the first place. She'd finally figured out she only hated him because of the way he made her feel.

Safe.

He made her feel safe. And no one, for years, had made her feel that way.

It wasn't even as if they had any interaction outside of their small group. Anthony was Logan and Brandon's friend. So when they got together, he was usually there. Just something about having him near, always made her feel safe. It was like when he walked in the door, a shield went up around her and nothing bad would happen. There was no other way to explain.

Damn if she'd tell him that though.

She knew through Mel's interference that Anthony liked her. That didn't mean a thing though. She wasn't into relationships and love and white picket fences. No matter how much her heart ached for those things.

Falling in love meant giving someone total control over your heart. And that meant, at any time, they could squeeze it in their hands and crush it into pieces.

Nope. No thank you.

Not for her.

She took another drink of vodka from the bottle. The alcohol made her fuzzy and pictures of Anthony flashed through her head like a slideshow.

Anthony up on a ladder fixing the security system, jeans so snug she wasn't sure how he even walked. Anthony, wearing only low-slung boardshorts with water cascading down his chest. Anthony grinding up against her at the bar when she'd purposely tried to torture him.

She moaned, not able to control it. The man was seriously hot. Tall, at least six foot five and lean. She was no short waif and he towered over her five foot eight, one hundred and fifty-pound body. She'd never felt small around a man but when she had danced with Anthony, she'd felt tiny. Maybe that was why she felt safe with him.

And wasn't that the crux of her problem? She didn't want to feel safe with anyone. Feeling safe meant she would let her guard down and, in letting her guard down, it was possible someone like Anthony would squeeze his way in.

For as big as he was, she had no problem imagining he was the one person who could wedge his way into even the tiniest of spaces.

She wanted to hate him. Had tried. But he was so headstrong and arrogant. He was also caring and sweet and damn if that wasn't annoying. While it seemed he loved to pick on and make fun of her, he stood up for her whenever anyone else did the same.

It felt nice that someone outside her family and friends stuck up for her.

That was part of the reason he made her feel safe; safe enough that she had let the damn man into her dreams. And she used the word "let" loosely. It seemed whether she wanted to or not, her sleeping brain and body only wanted Anthony.

For months, all of her dreams and fantasies had included him. It had gotten so bad, she was even thinking about him when she was awake. And that was bad. Bad, bad, bad. When she started imagining him while wide awake, she knew it was time to somehow, someway purge him from her life.

She had no idea how she was going to go about doing that. Not when he was friends with Logan and Brandon and always seemed to be around. But it was a must. If she wanted to stick to her guns and never give her heart away, Anthony had to go. And soon.

Sunday morning dawned and Carly woke up startled. She had fallen asleep on the couch after finishing the bottle of vodka and she was paying for it. Her head was pounding and it hurt to open her eyes. Hangovers were unfortunately something she woke up with when she overindulged, unlike both Leah and Melanie who woke up completely fine.

It was exasperating as fuck.

"I see someone had a good time last night?"

Carly turned at the words and saw Leah, hands-on-hips, staring at her.

Flopping back down on the couch, she covered her eyes with her arm. "What the hell are you doing here?"

She heard Leah move further into the house and walk past the couch where she was lying. Instead of answering the question, Leah asked, "How much did you drink?"

Blindly searching the floor next to the couch, she held up the empty vodka bottle. "All of this."

"Well then, that explains the phone calls."

Her body stiffened and she dropped her arm which had been covering her eyes and opened them. "What phone calls?" She had a horrible feeling about this.

Walking toward her, Leah handed her a bottle of water and some ibuprofen. "The three phone calls at two in the morning which I didn't get until I woke up this morning."

Swallowing the pills with the water, she asked. "What did I want?"

Leah's eyebrows raised and she scrunched up her face. "It might be easier if I just play them for you." Taking her phone out, she hit play on Carly's first message.

"Is it possible to go insane from lack of sex. I think it might be happening to me. Like no joke, I am seeing visions, but the fucking problem is, all the visions are of Anthony. And I don't want to have visions of Anthony. I want to not have visions of Anthony. Did I say that right? And also, that's a lie. I want to have more than visions of Anthony. I want that man with his head between my thighs making me scream his name from the top of my lungs. And you know how loud I am. The whole fucking town would hear it."

The recording stopped and the room was silent. She looked up at Leah and cringed. "That's not horrible, right?"

"It gets worse." She hit play on the next message.

"How bad would it be if I just slept with him once? Once wouldn't be so bad, would it? He can't be that good that it would break me. Nobody's that good. Sex that is so all-consuming is a myth. It's a unicorn. It does not exist. So once would be okay and then I could be done with him. In all likelihood, I won't even want it more than once."

"Oh shit." She dropped her head into her hands. Everything she had said to Leah in the message was what she had been thinking.

"There's one more," Leah said and before Carly could tell her she didn't want to hear it, she hit play.

"I did it. I called Anthony and told him I wanted to have sex with him. The ball is in his court." When the room went silent again, Carly did the only thing she could think of. She grabbed her phone and searched her outgoing calls.

And she did not like what she saw.

"I called him four times," she whispered.

Leah took the phone out of her hand. "He didn't call back so maybe he hasn't heard the messages yet?"

"Is my life the plot of a romantic comedy? I'm supposed to what...go to his house and get to his phone before he does so I can erase the messages?"

"Don't yell at me. I'm just trying to look on the bright side."

Carly took a deep breath and tried to calm down. "I know. And I'm sorry. I just...I can't believe I did this."

"I kinda can," Leah said.

At her confused look, Leah explained. "Your feelings for Tony have been building up for so long, Carls. This was inevitable. You can't just force feelings down and hope they go away. That's not the way it works."

"It is in my world," she answered honestly.

Leah put a hand on her leg. "I know you really believe love isn't worth it. At least for you. But take it from me, it is. And to answer your question from your second message, it's not a unicorn. Sex can be that good, especially when you are in love."

Carly gave Leah a dirty look. "How many times have I told you that I do not want to hear about your sex life with my cousin."

"There's my girl," Leah said. "I knew you couldn't stay away too long."

Carly rolled her eyes and leaned back on the couch. "What do I do now?"

"My suggestion, deal with this head-on. Call him back and explain that you were drunk and sad and horny and it was a mistake." She looked at Carly, her head tilted. "Unless, you don't want it to be a mistake?"

Did she? Obviously her drunk mind had spoken the truth but was she ready to face that truth? More importantly, would she really be able to sleep with Anthony just one time? Her feelings for him seemed to get stronger every day. Even though she spent a lot of time trying to refute them, she was never able to.

"I don't know what I want to do. I know something is going to have to give or else I am going to have to give up alcohol. Because drunk dialing is for people with no self-control. And I have self-control."

Leah laughed. "Yeah, I can see that. You're just full of self-control."

"Shut up," Carly said

"Why'd you drink so much last night?"

Carly shrugged. "I was just lonely." It was hard to admit, but Leah was her friend and wouldn't judge her.

"The fuck, Carls, if you were lonely why didn't you tell me or Mel. You are always welcome to come hang out with either of us."

"I don't want to be a third wheel. You guys deserve some alone time."

"It's not as if we're gonna have sex on the dining room table while you're there. Jeez."

"I know that but I hate being the odd man out."

"You know, if you dated, you wouldn't always be the third wheel."

"You know why I'm not dating." Months ago, Carly had tried going out on dates and even just picking up guys for sex, but her tries had failed when all she could think about was Anthony.

"Then maybe you should date Tony."

Closing her eyes, she said, "You know why I can't."

"No, not really. I know why you think you can't. But that's not a real reason. One broken heart seven years ago is not a reason not to try again, especially when you already know the guy likes you."

"Really? One broken heart seven years ago. You know it wasn't as simple as that. My freaking mom was sleeping with my boyfriend, Leah. That is not a commonplace broken heart. That's Jerry Springer shit."

"Okay, I'm gonna ask a question and I want you to really think about it. And remember, I was there, so I have an opinion. Think back on your feelings for Rob, before he cheated. Were they even a fraction of the feelings you have for Tony?"

Her immediate thought was to say yes. She had loved Rob, or at least loved him as much as a twenty-year-old girl could love. But before she answered, she remembered those safe feelings she got whenever Anthony was around. Those feelings were so much more defined and prominent than the feelings of love she'd had for Rob.

Did that mean something? Had she not really loved Rob?

"By your silence, I see you are taking the time to think this through. Let me tell you what I saw though. I saw a girl, a young woman, that was so desperate for love because her mom never cared about her. So when the big man on campus asked you out, you jumped at the chance. And for a while, you were happy. But don't you remember, right before you caught him with your mom you were thinking about breaking up with him? You said that while the sex was good, you didn't really care about him. Then you found him with your mom and from there on out, what should have been a blip in your dating history, became the defining moment that would hold you back the rest of your life."

Leah's words penetrated her mind. She saw the clear picture that she was trying to make and then all of a sudden she recalled making the decision to break up with Rob. How had she forgotten?

"Why did you never tell me this before?"

"Before you weren't ready, and you weren't in love." She shrugged nonchalantly. "Now you are."

"I'm not in love with Anthony," she defended as Leah stood and walked to the door.

"Keep telling yourself that," she said as she opened the door. "Come over for dinner tonight. No arguing." The door closed behind her and Carly could only stare at the empty air where Leah had just stood.

Leah was wrong. She wasn't in love with Anthony.

Just because she had feelings for him – strong feelings – that wasn't love.

Was it?

Chapter 2

Moving slowly, Tony opened his front door and punched in the code to his alarm system to disarm it. He was exhausted and all he wanted was a flat surface to fall onto for a minimum of eight hours of sleep.

One of the businesses his company secured had been broken into ,and at midnight he'd had to go down to the office to run through the security footage with the police. It was tedious work and took hours but was part of his job as the owner of a company.

Bypassing his couch, he walked down the hall to his bedroom. He figured it would be darker in there and that might help him sleep for a longer period of time.

He had just laid down when he felt something under his back. Lifting up, he reached his hand under his body and felt around until he came out with his cell phone.

"So that's where it was," he said out loud. It wasn't until he had gotten to his office that he realized he'd left it at home.

He was reaching out to drop it on his nightstand when it caught his eye that he had four missed calls. Sighing, he brought the phone back to his face to check the messages. Missed calls in the middle of the night or on a weekend meant only one thing; those eight hours of sleep he desperately needed were probably not going to happen.

Swiping his finger across the screen, he froze in shock when he saw who the missed calls were from.

Carly.

All four were from Carly, at two in the morning.

That could only mean one thing. Something was wrong.

He hit play on the first message, standing up at the same time. If something was wrong, he needed to go, right then and there.

Her voice stopped him cold.

"I've decided we should have sex. I mean, why are we waiting? We both want to, right? I know I do. Man do I. It's killing me to hold back and act like I hate you. Your body, holy shit, have you looked in a mirror because you are seriously ripped and I just want to devour you. Soon. Call me back."

He blinked and adjusted his growing cock in his pants. Had she really just said all that and then ended with 'call me back'. What the fuck?

Pressing play on the next message, he listened intently.

"Why are you not calling me back? I'm so horny even just the smallest touch from you would make me come. That reminds me, I am dying to have your head between my legs. Do you know every night when I use my vibrator, that's the image I conjure up? You eating me out, sucking my clit until I come all over your face. God, this is turning me on more. Please call me."

He swallowed the lump in his throat. He could tell by her voice she was drunk. She always talked in rambling sentences, but when she drank, it got worse. Her words were so clear and defined though. It was like she had thought of them before.

Little did she know the image which made her come every night was the same one he jerked off to every day. Tasting her was becoming an obsession.

Sitting down, before he fell over from lack of blood to his brain, he pressed play on the next message.

"Anthony," she breathed out heavily and almost had him coming. "Please, I need you."

That was the whole message and in his mind, he imagined she was playing with herself. Her voice had been full of heat and almost sounded like a moan.

Hitting play on the last message, he held his breath.

"I'm lonely," she sobbed out. "I'm so lonely. And I don't want to be lonely anymore."

When the message ended, he finally breathed. He was horny, confused and sad all at the same time. She sounded so sad in her last message. And, if he knew Carly—and he was beginning to think he did—she would hate that. She was not in the business of being vulnerable in front of people.

He understood loneliness though. He felt it too. Sure he had his mom, dad and sister. But at thirty-five, most of his friends were married and that meant he didn't see them very often. Then he met Carly, and on that day it was like the Earth opened up and swallowed everyone and everything, but her. He wasn't a person who believed in fate and happily ever after. He'd thought if it was real it would have already happened to him. He was never so happy to be so wrong.

She was magnificent and he could hardly think straight when he wasn't with her. It was like she was his lifeline. When he was near her, he felt calm on the inside. But apart from her, which was more often than not, he felt panicked.

There was no other way to explain it other than with love.

And that had thrown him for a giant loop.

How could he possibly love her when he'd barely spent any time with her? To figure it out, he'd made it a point to go around her more. And it only got worse. She was bossy, condescending, and arrogant. He fucking couldn't get enough.

A masochist is what he was.

Then he'd catch a glimpse of her soft side. She loved her friends and both Logan and Brandon fiercely. That meant something to him. Not to mention the way she was with the kids she taught at her studio. They worshipped her. Listening to every word she said, their eyes gleaming when she danced.

If he'd learned anything in his thirty-five years of life it was that kids were a good judge of character. And that meant his bossy woman was also an amazing woman.

His woman.

Yeah, he knew it wasn't true. Yet. But he'd give his left arm to make it true.

Those messages though. They were so unlike the Carly he knew. And, if he had to guess, as soon as she remembered she called him, she would be mortified.

Needing to hear her voice again, he started at the beginning and listened to the messages. On his third listen through, he had no choice but to pull his dick out and stroke himself. Her voice talking about his head between her legs was torture. He wanted the same thing, but, if he couldn't have it, he had to at least relieve some of the pressure before he caused serious damage to himself.

Stroking himself up and down, he tuned in to her breathy moans and panting. Within seconds his release covered his hand and stomach, as he groaned out her name.

Breathing heavy, he grabbed a shirt off the floor to clean up the mess. All the exhaustion he'd felt just thirty minutes ago was gone, replaced by a euphoria that maybe, just maybe, Carly was ready for more.

How should he handle this situation though? Should he lie and say he never received the messages? Would she even believe that? No, he couldn't do that to her. Not to mention, he hated lying. It was messy and people always tripped up.

That basically left confronting it head-on. What he could do though, is play it off like no big deal, hopefully making her feel better about herself.

Grabbing a new shirt, he pulled it on and headed down the hallway. It was eleven and even though Carly had obviously drunk the previous night, she should be up. He had just grabbed the keys to his truck when there was a knock on his door.

Pulling it open, he found his sister, Addie.

"I expected you to be sleeping." She strolled in like she owned the place. He loved his sister, he truly did. But right then, he had more important things on his mind.

"If you thought I would be asleep, then why the hell are you here?" He shut the door, resigning himself to the fact he was going to have to talk to her before he could go see Carly.

He followed her to his small kitchen where she had turned on his Keurig and was picking a pod for brewing.

"I had breakfast with mom and dad. Dad mentioned one of our clients had a theft and you were up all night dealing with it."

"I was, but that still doesn't explain why you are here when you thought I would be sleeping."

"Why didn't you call me to help?" She was leaning against the counter and her expression told him she wasn't mad so much as annoyed.

Raising his eyebrows, he asked, "You wanted me to call you at midnight to go through hours of footage?"

"Yes." She hit the start button on the coffee machine. "You promised I could have more of a role in the company, Tony."

Not this again. He'd been training her to do more and more around the office and while at first he had hesitated, now he was beginning to think she had a knack for it. But that didn't mean he was ready to hand the reins of his company over to her.

"Addie, you're doing a great job, better than I ever thought, if I'm being honest. But do you really want to take the calls that come in during the middle of the night?"

"I want to be valuable; have a purpose." She sipped her now brewed coffee. "One day I am hoping you will meet a nice woman and then you won't want to take the calls that come in during the middle of the night either."

He ran a hand through his dark, almost black hair. "I own the company, Add. I'm always going to be taking calls in the middle of the night. Won't matter if I have someone in my life."

"That's just it. You don't have to if you share the burden with me."

He wondered why he was even arguing with her. He hated middle of the night calls and here she was saying she wanted to do them. He needed his head checked.

"All right, from now on, we will alternate calls that come in during the night. Will that make you happy?"

She nodded firmly. "Yes." She eyed him critically. "Now, tell me what you are doing up?"

He shook his head. "Why wasn't I an only child?"

Laughing, she punched his arm. "Your life would be so boring without me."

"A repercussion I could totally deal with."

"Tell me there's a woman. Please, please tell me there's a woman."

Figuring it was either talk to her or kill her, he opted to talk. "There's a woman."

"Whoop!" she shouted. "I knew it. I need details." She sat down at his table, making it known she wasn't budging until she had info.

"Her name is Carly." He pulled out a chair and sat too.

"I'm gonna go ahead and assume she is in the group of friends you have been hanging with?"

"She's Logan's cousin." He and Logan had been friends a long time, and over the years, Addie had met him several times.

"No way. Is he cool with that?"

Was Logan cool with Tony being ninety percent in love with Carly? He had no real fucking clue. They had skirted the issue some, and Brandon knew because Tony had let it slip, but guys weren't in the habit of talking about their feelings.

On the other hand, Melanie knew, and since she and Logan were together, that most likely meant Logan knew.

He shrugged. "I think he knows enough."

"So are you like dating this girl, or what?"

"I'm done talking about this. Why don't you go bother someone else."

She pouted. "You're no fun."

He examined his sister. She was beautiful – he'd been told that enough through the years. Yet, she rarely dated or even hung out with friends. He knew for a fact though she wasn't shy or timid.

"Are you dating anyone?"

She looked down at her coffee mug. "Dating is hard."

He was familiar with what she was saying, and while he in no way wanted to hear about her dating life, she was young and should be out having fun.

"What about friends? I never hear you talk about anyone anymore?"

"I don't really have any friends." Her admission stunned him.

"That can't be. You are a friendly, happy person. Not to mention gorgeous."

"I think it's the last one that makes me a bad friend."

"What? What does being gorgeous have to do with having friends?" This whole conversation was beyond confusing to him.

She blew out a breath. "Girls are weird about having a pretty friend. They think all guys want me and that makes me a bad friend." Her mouth was turned down in a frown.

"Someone said that to you?" He was pissed that someone could be so rude.

"Yes and no. It's just something I've learned to live with. In high school, it was the reason I only ever hung out with those snooty girls. They were the only ones accepting of me. I really wanted to hang out with the math and computer geeks."

Tony was disgusted to the point of wanting to vomit. He'd had no idea his lively happy sister had gone through any kind of discrimination. And to do it because people thought she was too pretty? That just flabbergasted him.

So much so, he wanted to do something about it. And he knew just what to do.

Ushering his sister out of his house, he jumped in his truck and headed for Carly's. No longer was he thinking about what he was going to say to her or how their conversation would go. Right then, he wanted her help. Addie deserved friends. Real friends. He'd spent enough time with Carly, Leah and Melanie to know they would never judge a person by their looks. And the more he thought about it the more he knew his sister would fit in perfectly with their group.

Pulling into Carly's driveway, he got out and was immediately greeted by Carly's dog, Max.

"Hey buddy." He patted his head and scratched behind his ears. Max followed him as he walked up the drive and stepped onto the porch. Before he could knock, the front door opened and Carly stood before him.

Sometimes, when he looked at her he had to remind himself to breathe. This was one of those times. Anyone else who looked at her would see a half put together, mess of a woman. He only saw her. He saw how tired she looked and the worry in her eyes over what he was doing there.

Before she could speak or freak out, he said, "I need your help with my sister."

He saw the second she registered what he said. "You have a sister?"

He tried to hide his smile. Of course that would be the first thing she would say. "I do."

She stepped back into the house. "Want to come in?" There was wariness in her voice, but he wasn't sure if it was because she didn't want him to come in or, because she did.

He nodded and walked past her, Max following on his heels. Not sure whether he should sit or stand, he turned and waited for her.

She also seemed unsure, which was a complete one-eighty from how she normally acted.

"How about we sit in the kitchen," she said. "Do you want some coffee or water?"

"Coffee would be great." He followed her and took a seat at the table.

"How old is your sister?" She was grabbing mugs from the cabinet.

"Twenty-six."

"How do you have a twenty-six-year-old sister none of us have met?"

"Well, Logan's met her and so has Melanie."

Her eyes went wide with shock. "Mel met her? When?"

Oh shit. He'd really stepped in it now. Melanie had met Addie when she'd come to his office to ask about his feelings for Carly. Only Tony didn't know how much of that story Carly knew. He knew Mel had told Carly some of it, but how much, he had no idea.

"Yeah, Addie, Addison," he corrected, "works with me at the office. Mel met her there."

She nodded slowly as if trying to figure out why Mel would have been at his office. Walking to the table, she handed him a cup of coffee and sat across from him with her own.

"So what kind of help do you need with your sister?"

"She needs friends. Real friends. And I was wondering if maybe you and Leah and Mel would be willing to be her friends?"

Coffee cup halfway to her mouth, she stopped. "You want me to be friends with your sister?"

"I guess I should start at the beginning?"

"Probably a good idea."

"Addie is a really pretty girl. Gorgeous actually. She always has been, and apparently, it's been torture."

"Wait," she interrupted him before he could go on. "How gorgeous? Like supermodel gorgeous or I live in a small town gorgeous. Cause they are two separate things."

He pulled his phone out and flipped through his pictures until he found one to show her.

"Holy shit." She took the phone out of his hand. "This is your sister?" She stared, slack-jawed at him.

"That's Addison."

"I thought you had to be biased when you said she was gorgeous, but she's seriously beautiful. Is she even wearing makeup?" She held the phone closer to her face.

"She's not really a girly girl, at least not anymore, so she's probably not wearing makeup."

"Wow, I kinda hate her. I have to shovel it on just to pass as presentable."

He scoffed. "Right."

"You think I'm joking? I rarely go out without at least some makeup on."

He scrutinized her. "You're not wearing makeup now."

"Yeah, and if I went out like this, I would scare the whole town."

He looked up at her, made sure to make eye contact. "You don't scare me." His voice was raw and he barely recognized it.

She held his gaze, and for a second, time stopped. He was afraid to speak or even breathe. He wanted the moment to go on forever. But, of course, it couldn't.

She broke the trance. "So back to your sister. Why does she need friends?"

He closed his eyes to gain some control and then opened them back up and went on with his story. "Apparently, it's a thing that girls don't like to have pretty friends." He paused to let her try and figure out what he was saying. Watching her mind work was one of his favorite things.

She started to speak but stopped and stood up. Hands-on-hips, she looked at him. "Are you saying she doesn't have friends because a bunch of bitches think she is too hot for them?" He was ready to answer her, but, in true Carly fashion, she kept going. "Because if that is what you are saying, then I'm gonna need some names. Women don't ever demean other women. Ever. And because they aren't secure enough in themselves and the way they look…Oh no. No, no, no."

He could only stare and watch her rant on his sister's behalf. She was unstoppable and the fact that she was standing up for someone she had never even met, proved to him that she was the woman he thought she was.

He wanted to tell her she was beautiful in her anger. That her heart, which was angry for someone else, was the best part of her. But he couldn't. Not yet.

Reaching for her phone, she started doing something on it. "I'm gonna friend her right now on Facebook and invite her to dinner tonight."

"You and I are not even Facebook friends." He smiled. He'd wanted to friend her a dozen times, but figured she wouldn't accept.

"Then I'll friend you too." And sure enough, his phone which was sitting on the table between them, lit up with a new friend request.

"Does she have a boyfriend, because she can bring him too?"

"No boyfriend." She was typing away on her phone and not looking at him. "Do I get to be invited to dinner?"

Her fingers stopped moving and she looked up at him. "Do you want to come to dinner?"

"A guy's gotta eat." He kept it light and hoped his voice and face didn't give him away. He wanted to shout YES he wanted to go to dinner, or anywhere else where she was. But again, he waited.

She studied him for a few minutes and silence enveloped them. When she finally spoke, concern was in her voice.

"Why do you look like you are about to fall asleep right there in your chair?"

It was the last thing he had expected her to say.

"I've been awake for," he glanced at his watch, "going on thirty hours now."

Her eyes widened in shock. "Why would you be awake that long?"

"There was a security issue at a business I cover and I got called in at midnight."

"You must be exhausted. You should go home and get some sleep. Better yet, sleep here. You shouldn't be on the road as tired as you are."

He was touched that she was so concerned. "I can drive home."

"No," she shook her head. "Stay here. Please."

It was the please that did it. Carly rarely asked nicely. She was a demanding person and liked getting her way. So, her saying please, meant something, at least to him.

Nodding once, he stood. "Okay. I am basically a zombie right now. The sooner I can sleep, the better."

She walked quickly around the table. "Bed or couch? There's still a bed in Mel's room, or you can use mine. It doesn't really matter."

She was nervous and it made him wish he wasn't so fucking tired. "The couch is perfect. I sleep on mine all the time." He followed her out of the kitchen and into the living room. Sitting down, he kicked off his shoes.

She stood, like a statue at the foot of the couch. "Umm, do you need a blanket or something?"

If the 'or something' was her, then yes, he would take that. Instead he said, "A blanket would be good."

She handed him one and he laid back, covering his legs with it. "Thank you for this. As soon as I close my eyes, I will be out."

"Sleep as long as you need."

He watched as she walked away and his eyes began to close.

He was taking a nap on Carly's couch.

Was there anything stranger?

Chapter 3

What in the fucking world had she been thinking? Anthony was asleep on her couch. Right in the middle of her living room where she had no choice but to look at him.

Technically she had a choice. She could go up to her room or outside, but neither of those things were happening when she had the chance to watch him sleep.

And, of fucking course, he looked like a movie hero doing it. She had no idea what she looked like sleeping. But if she had to guess, it was not pretty. And there was most definitely drool involved. But not with him. He looked peaceful, happy and drool free.

Who looked happy when they slept?

Needing some space from the hot guy sleeping on her couch, she grabbed her phone and crept through the house so she could go outside on her porch. She tried to get Max to go with her, but he'd suddenly taken a liking to Anthony, and chose to sleep by the couch. Traitor.

Sitting down on the swing, she replayed the story about Addie. She, of course, had known mean girls in her life. But none so bad they'd refused to be friends with someone because of their beauty. Sure, sometimes a girl just wasn't your cup of tea and you made the decision not to have them as a friend. But a nice girl? And she had no doubt his sister was nice. If she was anything like him, she was probably perfect. And while she hated that quality in him, in a friend she didn't care.

Checking her phone she saw she had a new message.

Addison:

Hi Carly, it's so nice of you to reach out and invite me to dinner. But, I have to ask...did Tony put you up to this? It's his style, always trying to fix everything.

Carly:

He didn't put me up to anything. He mentioned he had a sister (for the first time, I might add) and I suggested it would be nice to meet you. I could use another comrade in arms against all the coupling up that is going on.

Addison:

I'm with you there. If I see anyone else making out in front of me, I might puke. Possibly on them.

Carly:

Well, then you might want to wear a blindfold at dinner. Leah and Brandon tend to forget the rest of us are there.

She typed out Leah and Brandon's address and told her to come around five. It was only after she did, that she realized she hadn't even asked Leah if it was okay.

Carly:

Is it okay if 2 more join us for dinner?

Leah:

Sure. Anyone I know?

Carly:

Anthony, and his sister, Addison

Leah:

Tony has a sister?

Carly:

It seems so.

Leah:

If Tony is coming to dinner, does that mean you two talked?

Carly:

Not about the messages. I'll tell you the whole story tonight.

Needing a nap herself, she went back inside, and up to her room. Maybe after she cleared some of the fog from her brain she would be able to figure out why Anthony never brought up her calls.

She woke with a start, to what sounded like a car door. Looking out her window, she saw Anthony's truck backing out of her driveway. A quick glance at the bedside clock told her it was just after three.

He was probably going home to shower and change before dinner, and if she was smart, she would do the same. After all, she was meeting his sister for the first time and she wanted to make a good impression.

For what reason, she had no idea.

After a quick shower, she dressed in her favorite pair of jean capris and a tank. It was September in Ohio, and they lived on a lake. Because of that, it could get cool so she also grabbed a cute jean jacket. She wanted to get to Leah and Brandon's early so she and Leah could talk.

She shouldn't have been surprised to find Logan's Jeep at Leah and Brandon's. Of course, Leah would call Mel, and have Logan and her over for dinner too.

She found them all outside on the deck, relaxing. The girls were sipping margaritas and Bran and Logan both had beer.

"I see the party started without me." She took a seat next to Mel and stole her drink.

"I kinda thought you'd have been here earlier," Leah said. "What the hell took you so long?"

"I took a nap, and by the time I woke up, there was just enough time to shower and get dressed."

"Hey Logan," Mel said sweetly. "I love you, but get lost."

Logan scoffed and looked at Brandon. "Do you see how she treats me?"

"Don't worry," Leah said. "Bran will keep you company."

"Kicked off my own deck," Brandon said with no real anger and stood. He bent to kiss Leah just as Logan did the same to Mel and then they were gone.

Pouring herself another margarita, Mel asked, "Leah tells me Addison is coming to dinner. And Tony. How'd that happen?"

"Wait, wait, wait." Leah said, both arms thrown in the air. "No talk of the sister until I know what happened with the calls?"

Carly sighed. "I'm assuming Leah filled you in?" she said to Melanie.

"Oh yeah, and might I just say. HOLY GODDAMN SHIT! I think I got a little wet listening to those messages so I can only imagine what happened to Tony if what you said to him was even half as hot."

Carly did not get embarrassed. Usually. But, right then, she felt her cheeks burn hot.

"Talk, and fast," Leah said. "We don't have much time."

"I don't think we talked or that I even left him any messages."

"That's not possible. You had to have left messages," Leah said. "The first two calls were like thirty seconds and the next two were like twenty. That means you left a message."

"I'm not an idiot," she said. "But he never mentioned it."

"Time out," Mel said. "What happened when you talked this morning?"

"He showed up at my house a little before eleven, and the first thing he said to me, was that he needed my help with his sister. That was it. No 'hey you left me four really racy messages last night, wanna go screw.'"

"OMG, you sounded just like him there." Melanie was dying with laughter.

"I don't see Tony saying screw though," Leah added. "Maybe fuck."

"People...can we stay on track?"

"Sorry," they said in unison.

Carly shook her head and tried not to laugh. She could always count on her friends to keep things easy and not let her get in her own head.

"After that, I invited him in and we talked about his sister, who I think we are all going to love."

"Just to backtrack, he said nothing about the calls?" Leah asked. "And you didn't bring them up?"

"Do I look crazy? No, I didn't bring them up."

"He got them," Mel said, and both she and Leah looked at her. "Don't you find it a little coincidental he just so happens to show up at your house the morning after you drunk dial him? Come on. He got them, but he just doesn't want to be the one to bring them up. So he concocted this sister thing to talk to you."

Carly looked from Mel to Leah. "Do you think that could be true?"

Leah shrugged. "Seems plausible."

Carly closed her eyes and sat back in the chair. If that was the case, then what had she said to him? Was it bad and that's why he didn't want to bring it up? Or, was it because he didn't want the same things?

"Before you have a nervous breakdown over there," she heard Mel say. "Are you gonna tell us what the deal is with Addison?"

She opened her eyes and looked out at the lake. Because it was September, most of the tourists were gone but the lake was still plenty busy with locals out on their boats.

"You met her, right?" she said to Mel. "Is she as gorgeous in person as she was in the picture I saw?"

"Yep." She pursed her lips. "I remember being a little jealous for you when I walked in and saw her in the office. She looked really young too. Like maybe just out of college."

"She's twenty-six."

"Holy cow, I need to know what she does to her skin."

"So what's the deal, and why did Tony need your help with her?" Leah asked, ignoring Mel.

"It seems she doesn't have a lot or maybe any friends because – and this part really pisses me off – girls don't want to be friends with her because of how she looks."

She waited for it to come, knew it would, because after all, they were her friends.

"Are you fucking kidding me?" Mel sat forward almost spilling her margarita.

"What she said," Leah added. "Girls are bitches."

"I was outraged when he said it. I just…fuck I know there are shitty people out there, but…" She trailed off and shook her head.

"This is a no-brainer then," Leah said. "We will be her friends."

"Agreed." Mel put her glass up, toast style. She and Leah clinked Mel's glass, and then Leah stood.

"I better go check on dinner."

"We'll join you," Carly said. "Addison should be here soon anyway."

"And Tony," Mel said following her. "Don't forget about him."

As if she ever could.

When they went into the house, Logan and Brandon were nowhere in sight.

"Where are the guys?" Carly asked.

"Probably in the office," Leah said as she checked on dinner.

Carly poured herself another drink and sat down at the bar. "Anthony slept on my couch today." She said it quietly, wondering if her friends were even paying attention to her. When Leah dropped the fork she was holding, she figured they had heard her.

"You've been here twenty minutes and you are just now telling us this?" She bent to pick up the fork from the floor.

"I wasn't sure if it meant anything."

"Why did he sleep on your couch and where were you while he was sleeping?" Melanie was practically chomping at the bit waiting for her answer. But before she could say anything, there was a knock at the door.

"Dammit," Mel said, and slammed her hand down on the counter. "Now I have to wait to have answers."

"You'll survive." Leah patted her shoulder as she walked past to go answer the door.

Carly was nervous. So nervous her leg wouldn't stop shaking. It wasn't as if she didn't spend a lot of time with Anthony, so why was she nervous? It didn't make sense to her.

She looked up and spotted him walking in the house. She was slightly aware of his sister standing next to him, but all she saw was him. All of a sudden, she wasn't nervous anymore. A calm came over her and her heartbeat slowed.

Damn him for making her feel safe.

She watched as he introduced his sister. Deciding she should probably join in, she stood and walked toward them.

"And this is Carly," he said when she was almost in front of him. "Carly, my sister Addie."

"Addison," she corrected him. "I told you to stop calling me Addie." She looked at Carly. "I told him to stop calling me that. He only does it because he knows I hate it." She held out her hand and Carly shook it.

"Addison it is then." She really was beautiful; almost blindingly so. "Come on in and let's get you a drink. Anthony," Carly turned her head to look at him, "I think the guys are in Bran's office."

"You call him Anthony?" Addison asked when they got to the kitchen.

"Yes," Mel said. "It's super annoying."

"Margarita, wine, beer or something non-alcoholic?" Leah asked

"Definitely margarita." She took the glass Leah held out to her. "So why do you call him Anthony?"

She had to hand it to her, she wasn't shy. "That's his name, why can't I call him that?"

Addison shook her head. "It's just that no one, except our mom, calls him Anthony."

"I just don't see him as Tony. Anthony fits better."

"Hey, I'm not judging. I like Addison better than Addie, so I get it."

"Logan almost always calls me Melanie instead of shortening it to Mel. I guess it's a personal preference."

"Oh, Addison comes in and makes a valid point, and now you are totally fine with me calling him Anthony?" She smiled and shook her head. "You two are off my Christmas list."

"Does that mean I get to be on your Christmas list?" Addison said. "Because I love presents."

"Oh my God, where have you been my whole life?" Leah said. "And why haven't we been besties?"

The four girls laughed. Leah was right though. Addison really fit in great, and Carly had no problem liking her right away.

"Carly, will you go grab the guys?" Leah asked. "Dinner's almost ready."

"On it," she said, and took her re-filled drink and walked down the hallway. She spotted the guys before they spotted her. She stopped outside the doorway and just took in the scene. The three of them had their heads together looking at something on Bran's desk. Logan and Brandon were good looking guys. Of course, she was biased, since they were cousins, but Anthony, he made her heart race.

Stepping into the room, she said, "Hey boys, dinner's almost ready."

They all looked up, but it was Anthony who caught her eye. She felt completely naked with him staring at her even, though she was fully clothed.

"Great, I'm starving," Logan said.

Carly stood aside. Her cousins walked out of the room. It was just Anthony and her.

"Did you get my note?"

"Note?" she asked. Why was he so close, and why could she not think of anything else but kissing him?

"Yeah, I left you a note when I left today."

She blinked up at him. "You left me a note? What did it say?" He was practically standing right in front of her, his arm brushing against hers. Chills covered her whole body.

Voice low, he said, "Just that I would see you tonight and thanking you for the couch."

His moving lips put her in a trance. She couldn't look away; didn't want to. Before she could think better of it, words were coming out of her mouth.

"Are you ever going to mention my calls?"

His Adam's apple bobbed, and if she wasn't mistaken, his breathing got heavier.

"I—I wasn't sure what to say, or, if you even remembered calling me?" He looked embarrassed, and since he never looked embarrassed, it gave her strength. She was perverse that way.

"I wouldn't have known if I hadn't also called Leah. Apparently, I shouldn't drink vodka when I'm alone."

"Why were you drinking alone?" Leave it to him to ask the million-dollar question.

She shrugged and asked another question so she wouldn't have to answer him. Letting him in on all her secrets was not in the plan. "What did I say in the messages I left you?"

"That's not important."

She scrunched up her face. "It is to me."

"Seriously, don't worry about it."

"Why won't you just tell me what I said?"

He ran a hand over his face and through his hair. "If you really want to know, then listen to them." He handed her his phone and walked around her and down the hallway. She stood, holding his phone, unsure what to do.

Did she listen? Did she not listen? And, what did it mean that he'd kept them?

Curiosity got the better of her. Shutting the door to the room so no one else could hear, she pressed play on the first message.

Listening to herself tell Anthony what she wanted him to do to her was hot. What had he thought when he'd listened? Had he been turned on?

By the time all four messages played, she was in awe of herself. She was not a shy woman, but this was more than even she was used to. Who was that brazen woman and why couldn't she channel her whenever she needed?

Oh, that's right, Vodka.

She started to delete the messages, but at the last second, decided against it. It wasn't her phone, so it wasn't her choice. Opening the door, she moved down the hallway and back into the kitchen. Everyone was already seated at the table and the only open seat was, of course, next to Anthony.

She sat while everyone was plating their food and slid his phone over to him. Leah had gone easy and made chicken enchiladas and a salad. She filled her plate with salad and was just waiting on the enchiladas.

"Wanna hand me your plate? she heard Anthony ask.

She did as he asked and watched as he filled her plate with the delicious smelling food. She couldn't remember the last time someone had done that for her.

Was it wrong that she found it sexy?

Conversation flowed, Addison asked all kinds of questions while they did the same to her. They'd found out she had a math degree from Ohio State and worked for several years there at a job she hadn't really enjoyed. She'd moved back to her hometown of Woodridge two years ago, and began working with Anthony. She enjoyed the work because it was technical, and that was her thing. Anthony was training her to eventually do everything he did.

It was fun to watch the two of them together. They bickered, like she knew siblings did, from all her years of watching Brandon and

Logan. But their love, and more importantly respect for each other, was front and center.

Since it was Sunday, and everyone had to work the next morning, the night ended early and everyone went their separate ways. She wanted to head straight to bed when she walked in her front door, but then she remembered the note Anthony had mentioned he'd left her.

She wanted to see it.

Looking at both her table and kitchen counter, it was nowhere to be found. Then she noticed something on the floor under the table. It must have blown off when he'd walked out the door.

She bent to pick it up and stood to read it.

Carly,

Thank you for loaning me your couch. When I woke up, I found you asleep in your bed, and you looked so peaceful that I couldn't bear to wake you. I'll see you again in a few hours. Addison is excited, or at least it seems like it, from her message.

But, you never can tell from messages, can you?

Anthony.

She read it again and again, wondering what he was trying to say with his last line? Was he unsure of how to take her previous night's messages? She'd listened to them and to her there was only one way to take them. She wanted him. Badly.

Was that why he was mad when she had asked him about them?

She was going to find out, but not that night. First she needed sleep.

Tomorrow she would talk to him. Until then, dreaming would have to do.

Chapter 4

Tony kicked the covers off his body in his restlessness. You'd think he'd be tired after only three hours of sleep that afternoon but his thoughts kept drifting to Carly and sleep was no match for her.

She'd looked refreshed and beautiful at dinner and the way she just accepted Addie as one of the group so easily...well, if he hadn't been practically in love with her before, that would have been the icing on the cake.

Addie had been so happy on the way home, saying she couldn't wait to hang out with the girls again. That would be happening soon since Carly had invited her to lunch on Tuesday. Tony was happy for her. He'd known Carly and the other girls would love his sister. It still boggled his mind that other women didn't want to be friends with her.

Women.

Getting out of bed, since sleep seemed to be pointless, he walked down the hallway to his kitchen and grabbed a bottle of water. Back in his room, he picked up his phone, swiping it on. Hitting play on Carly's messages, he leaned back against his headboard and listened to her voice. He knew it was wrong, that he should delete them immediately, but that was damn near impossible. If this was as close as he would ever come to her wanting him, there was no way he was giving it up.

Hearing her voice, once again, had him hard as stone. He wanted nothing more than to grip his cock and release all the pressure building up. Yet, he didn't. Listening to the messages was one thing, but jerking off to them, again and again, was his line.

He wanted the real thing. And he was going to find a way to get it.

He turned his phone off and laid back down. He was almost asleep when his phone rang, startling him. Picking it up, he saw it was the police and he knew what that meant. Another sleepless night as he dealt with a client.

He spoke to the officer, who happened to be his friend Carl, and found out it was the same business as the previous night. He was just getting dressed when he remembered what his sister had asked him that morning.

She wanted more responsibility, and there was no time like the present.

He dialed her number and she picked up on the first ring.

"Tony what's wrong?" She sounded wide awake but then again, she hadn't been up all night the night before.

"There's a problem at Haskell's again. You want it?"

"Really? Heck yeah, I want it. Thank you for trusting me."

"You don't have to thank me. You earned it. But, if something comes up you can't handle, call me?"

"Absolutely," she said.

Tony hung up and once again laid back down. Maybe now he would finally be able to sleep.

When his alarm went off the next morning he was relieved Addie hadn't called him. His body and mind had needed a full eight hours and that was just what he got. Sitting up he turned and his feet landed on the floor. He had never been one of those people who hit snooze or relaxed in bed for a few more minutes. When the alarm went off, he got up.

After a shower and his first cup of coffee, he jumped in his truck and drove the three-point two miles to his office. His office sat in a strip of buildings in the center of town. He'd lived in Woodridge his whole life and after college, it had been a no-brainer for him to come home. He loved small-town life and didn't think that would change as he got older. Plus, Woodridge wasn't that small. It was the biggest small town in a fifty mile radius and they had shopping and restaurants galore.

Someone who lived in say, Cedarville, would come to Woodridge if they were looking for a night out at anything other than a local bar.

Parking his truck on the street in front of his office, he got out and walked up to the door. The lights were on and the door was unlocked meaning Addie was already there.

When he didn't see her he called out. "Morning."

She stepped out of his office looking energized. "Hey."

"Talk to me about last night," he said, bypassing all small talk. He walked into his office and she followed.

"The police caught the guy or I should say, woman." She was sitting on the edge of his desk smirking.

"It was a woman?" Not that Tony thought a woman couldn't commit crimes, he'd seen it plenty of times. It was just the situation seemed different.

"You're never going to believe it. Like seriously, you'd never guess in a million years." The excitement in her eyes had him smiling. She was such a strange creature.

"What if I don't guess and you just tell me?"

"It was the wife!" she blurted out. "Can you believe that? His own wife was breaking in and stealing from him."

Not much surprised him anymore when it came to his job, so he was not as shocked as Addie was. "And how'd you figure it out?"

"I caught her car pulling away on one of the cameras across the street."

"Good thinking." He'd have checked the other local cameras too and was happy she had thought of it.

"As soon as the police talked to her, she confessed. Said she was pissed at him for cheating on her and wanted him to pay. But, and get this, he was not cheating on her. He was planning a huge bash for her birthday in two weeks and had been covertly meeting with venues and planners for months."

Now that surprised him. "Wow." He shook his head. "Remind me to never throw anyone a surprise party."

Her eyes widened. "Not even Carly?" At the mention of her name, he felt his heart beat faster. And how fucking stupid did that make him feel? A man should not get all riled up just hearing a woman's name.

"Not if it meant she would ever think I was cheating on her," he finally said, answering honestly.

"Don't you think trust is a two-way street though? Why would Bob Haskell's wife ever think her husband was cheating? What has he done or not done in the past to make her that suspicious of him?" She raised her eyebrows. "I think that is the bigger problem."

She was probably right, although what did he know? Relationships had not really been his thing. But honesty was. He was always honest; something his dad had instilled in him at a young age. "Yeah, well, not everyone thinks like you do, Addie."

"Addison," she said forcefully and stood. "Call me Addison or, at my lunch with Carly tomorrow, I will tell her all your dirty little secrets."

"I don't have any dirty little secrets."

"Then I'll just make some up." She walked away, leaving him alone in his office. While he was telling the truth that he didn't have any secrets, he needed to remember to call her Addison. He did not want her making anything up and telling Carly.

He had enough roadblocks when it came to her.

He worked for about an hour before he stood up and walked out to the front. Addison was at her desk looking like the late-night had finally caught up with her.

"Go home," he said as he refilled his coffee.

"I'm okay," she said, her voice not convincing at all.

"Seriously, Add, go home. I'm headed out in a few anyway and there is nothing pressing that needs to be done right now. Go."

"Really? I hate to leave but, I am exhausted."

"Boss's orders. And don't come in till tomorrow." She was out the door within a few minutes and he had the office to himself. He wasn't joking when he'd said there was nothing pressing. Business was good but he had no new installs or any maintenance, and that meant it was all paperwork and bills. Not his favorite thing but something he had to get done.

That was why he had told Logan last week that he would stop over to his new art gallery and help with some general construction. Looking at his watch, he realized if he wanted to be there at the set time, he'd better leave.

On his drive to Cedarville, he couldn't help but think of Carly. What was she doing? Was she thinking of him at all? Was what she said in the messages real?

He knew they had to talk about them. It was not in her to let things go, and this was a big one. That meant he needed to initiate, and soon.

Entering Cedarville, he found a spot in the lot behind what would soon be Logan's gallery. It was a big space and Tony was glad his friend was doing something with it he loved. He saw Brandon standing by the back door when he got out of his truck.

"Logan rope you into helping too?" he said, as he walked toward Brandon.

"It seems I am required to spend all my free time here." Anyone who didn't know Brandon might think he sounded annoyed but Tony knew it was all just for fun. As brothers, Logan and Brandon really valued each other.

"I'm almost one hundred percent positive you don't spend all your free time here. If I know anything about women and admittedly it's not much, I know Leah would not want you gone all the time."

Together they walked in the back door of the building.

"You are so right. Thankfully, she loves me and has no problem being here herself helping out."

That sounded about right to Tony. The girls were tight and since Melanie probably spent a lot of time helping Logan, Leah would have no problem jumping right in.

"Where is this brother of yours?"

Tony looked around. It had been a week or so since he'd been inside and a lot of work had been done. A divider wall had been added to separate one section from another. Logan said a wall made for a better atmosphere when people were walking around.

Trust him to know.

They had also started on the offices, which were in the back. The place was really starting to look good.

Logan appeared from where the offices were. "Hey man, thanks for coming."

"Helping you is more fun than paperwork."

"That's why I hired someone to do that." Logan had hired his mom to run the gallery full time even though he would be living in town. He didn't want to deal with the day-to-day stuff like paperwork and payroll when he could be dealing with the artwork.

That was, after all, his thing.

"Point me in the direction you want me and I'll get to work."

Logan started walking and Tony and Brandon followed. "I'd like to work on some kind of counter here in the front. I don't want something huge, just something that could have a computer if any staff is out here and needs to get on it."

Tony appraised the area and started giving ideas. He'd worked in construction all through high school and college with a friend of his dads, so he knew his way around a project. This wasn't even work for him; more like fun.

They worked for hours, each of them helping out and pitching in where they could. They stopped for lunch when Melanie came by with sandwiches from the deli, but that was it. The next time they took a break, Tony looked at his watch and saw it was after seven.

"We've been working a while," he said to Logan.

"Yeah, I think it's probably time to call it a day." He set down his drill and stood back to look at the work they had been doing. "I think it's gonna look good."

"Yeah," Tony said and admired their work. "That stone countertop you got is going to really stand out."

"I hope so. I paid enough for it."

Brandon walked over, looking dusty and dirty. "Are we finished, because that drywall was a bitch." He'd been working in the offices for the last part of the day trying to get the walls put up.

Logan clapped him on the back. "Go on home to your lady. I'll clean up here."

"She's still at the dance studio, so it's not as if I have anything better to do."

"And since I don't have a lady, I can stay and help." Tony started picking up tools and putting them away.

"What's up with that?" Brandon asked from where he was sweeping up dust.

Giving him a quizzical look, he asked, "What's up with what?"

"You, not having a woman?" This from Logan who was standing over him looking down.

"That's not exactly what I was asking." Brandon stopped sweeping. "I was wondering what was up with you and Carly?"

"That too," Logan said with a headshake.

Tony stood and wiped his brow. "Nothing's happening. You see how she treats me."

"That's all fucking bullshit," Logan said. "She's deflecting. If she actually hated you, she'd just ignore you. The fact that you get under her skin means she likes you."

Tony laughed. "It's funny you should say that. Melanie told me virtually the same thing." She'd come to see him months ago, wondering what his feelings were for Carly. When he'd pointed out that it seemed as if she hated him, Melanie had said the same thing Logan had.

"If there's one person we know, it's Carly. She's been like a little sister to us and we know how she acts in most situations," Brandon said. "She's transparent when it comes to her feelings."

"Maybe to you, but to me...well, let's just say I feel like I am drowning most of the time trying to figure her out."

"Why the fuck didn't you say something," Logan said. "We can totally help you out with this."

Tony laughed. "I don't need any help. At least I hope not. She either wants to be with me or she doesn't. It's that simple." He hated talking about this. It made him feel like he was betraying her in some way, especially with her cousins; cousins who didn't seem to have any problem with them being together.

"You guys really don't care that I like Carly?"

Brandon threw his hands in the air. "If she ever gets the stick out of her ass, and realizes what is in front of her face, I will be a happy man. You are one of the best men I know, Tony, and I'd be proud to have you date my cousin."

"I feel the same," Logan said. "Not to mention, for some reason, she has been unhappy a long time and I am ready for her to be happy."

Tony was shocked and touched at their words. He had a sister, and while he thought both Logan and Brandon were great guys, he would in no way want them dating her. It was just the way it was.

Bro code.

"I'm glad to hear that," he shrugged, "but I'm not sure how much it's really going to matter."

"Don't give up on her," Brandon said. "She's hard-headed and stubborn as hell, but she needs someone in her life. And if that someone was you, even better."

"I don't plan on giving up, at least not anytime soon, but there is only so much a man can take."

"You know how fucking wishy-washy Melanie was when we first got together. I never knew if she was coming or going. It just takes time."

Tony knew it took time, but he knew Carly was not someone you could push. Deep down, he was in pain. And not just from his dick. Although that was there. This was a pain that could be stopped if she'd only acknowledge, to his face, that she liked him too. He needed those damn words from her. Needed her to ease his pain.

But, because he knew her well, he knew it wasn't going to come easy.

He left the gallery, and since he was starving, stopped at Gayle's to have a sandwich and a beer. Gayle's was a nice enough bar. They served food, making it even better. Since he'd been hanging with Logan and Brandon more, this seemed to be the place they went, more often than not.

Being a Monday meant it was busy with all the locals coming in to watch football and gather with their friends. He ate in silence at the bar and was content in doing so. He was just about to pay when a pretty woman slid onto the stool next to him. Because he'd been here enough, he recognized her.

"Are you leaving already?" she asked, her voice flirty and her eyes trained on his. "I was hoping to spend some time getting to know you?"

He wanted to roll his eyes. What a corny ass line. "Unfortunately, I have to get home."

"I'm Kristi," she reached her hand out for him to shake and he did.

"Tony," he answered.

"Are you sure you can't stay a little longer, Tony? I'll buy you a drink?"

He gave her a once over. She was pretty, really pretty with her long brown hair and body that looked like it spent hours in the gym to tone. It had been so long since he'd been with a woman and she obviously wanted him.

He could have sex with her, just this once, and it wouldn't be the end of the world. He wasn't in a relationship, after all. What was holding him back?

Carly.

Fuck.

Why was it so hard to get a woman, who didn't even seem to want him out of his head? And why was he staying celibate for her? For all he knew, she was sleeping with a different guy every night.

His heart fell.

Thinking of her sleeping with a different guy every night was too much. He had to get out of there.

"Kristi, it was nice to meet you, but I have to go." He didn't wait for her reply, just beelined out of the bar and straight to his truck. His mind was swirling with thoughts and images that were too much.

They were all too much.

Pulling out onto the road he drove on autopilot until he found himself in Carly's driveway.

He wasn't sure what he was doing there or what he planned to say or do, but he just knew he had to see her.

There were lights on, telling him she was home and when he knocked on the door, he wanted desperately to take it back.

He was a lunatic, coming here for no reason, just because the thought of her with other men had him on edge. She was an adult who was not in a relationship. She could do whatever she wanted.

But all that went out the window the second she opened her front door.

"Are you sleeping with other people?" he blurted. He couldn't even believe he'd said the words out loud.

She was beautiful standing before him with her dance outfit still on and her hair a rumpled mess on top of her head. She wore no make-up, and if he didn't know her, he'd think she was barely legal.

"Have I opened the door to an alternate universe or something? Oh I know, I'm on one of those hidden camera shows?" Her expression wasn't angry, more confused.

He tried to speak but only made it worse. "I just need to know who you're sleeping with."

She raised her eyebrows. "YOU need to know? What even gives you the right to ask? Plus, who in the ever-loving world asks anybody that? It's nobody's business."

He rubbed both his eyes with the heels of his hands. He was crazy. A certifiably crazy man. No wonder she didn't like him. If he was going to sound crazy then he might as well go all out.

"I can't even force myself to sleep with a woman when she hits on me because all my brain can think about is you. You consume every thought, every waking minute of my day."

She was breathing heavily, her chest rising and falling quickly, and her hand was covering her mouth. Her unreadable eyes stared him down.

"Say something," he whispered, unable to take the silence.

And then like always, she surprised him. "What about when you are asleep?"

He knew what she meant and closed his eyes, relishing in the fact that she had yet to slam the door in his face. "Those too."

When he reopened his eyes, they both stayed silent. It was the sound of her phone ringing that broke the spell.

"I have to get that," she said, making no move to walk away or close the door.

"I should go." He looked down at his feet before turning and walking away. He was just at the bottom of her porch when he heard her speak.

"There is no one." Her voice was soft yet forceful.

The phone had ceased ringing and Tony stopped in his tracks. Unsure of his next move, he stood there and tried to remain calm.

"I tried going out with other guys, but they weren't what I wanted."

He turned so fast it made his head spin. Her words echoed over and over in his head. If they weren't what she wanted, was she saying he was?

She stood in the doorway, darkness beginning to settle in around her. While the woman from the bar earlier was pretty, Carly was gorgeous. She was tall and lean, from dancing he suspected, and she carried herself in a way that let people know she had confidence.

He'd only met her twice before he'd accidentally walked in on her naked in her own bedroom. He had been doing a check to make sure his alarm system could not be breached, and he'd had no idea she was home. When he was eye level with her window, he found her completely naked, dripping with water, from what he assumed had been a shower.

She was exquisite.

It had taken every ounce of his control not to visibly peruse her naked form. But he saw it, couldn't not see it. Did she run and hide to cover up? No. She stood there, strong and determined, like it didn't bother her at all for him to see her naked.

If her nakedness hadn't made him want her, her attitude sure had.

He hadn't been the same since.

She was standing the same way now, strong and determined, just waiting for his next move.

Not able to deny either of them, he went up the steps two at a time before closing in on her. Right before his lips crashed down on hers she whispered "Anthony" and his legs just about gave out by how needy her voice sounded.

With the first touch of his lips to hers, it was like an explosion. She was soft and demanding and sweet, all at the same time. He couldn't get enough.

Her arms had gone around his neck and they were holding him to her like a vise. And since he had no plans to be anywhere but right there, he was okay with it.

His own hands found her ass and held her to him while his lips tasted and teased. She tasted like berries and lemons and since he knew that was the flavor of her favorite tea, he suspected she had just had some.

The kiss went on and on, neither of them letting go or making a move to take it further. It was just enough to finally admit their feelings for each other. Nothing else was needed.

Slowing his pace, he kissed down her neck to her ear.

"I just knew it," she whispered.

"Knew what?" His lips never left her skin as he spoke but she pulled back at his question. Her eyes were sadder than they should have been after a kiss.

"That you had the power to break me." There were tears forming in her eyes.

"Carly," he said and took her hand, "I would never hurt you."

"I know and none of this has anything to do with you. It's all my issue."

"Talk to me?" he pleaded. "Tell me what I can do?"

She half smiled and ran a hand down his chest. "I can't. Tonight. But I will, I promise." She took a step back from him. "Just...please don't give up on me yet."

He shook his head side to side slowly. "That would be impossible."

He gave her one last pleading look before turning and walking down the steps to his truck. Once inside, he started the engine and backed up quickly. He was positive, if after that kiss he didn't remove himself from her vicinity and fast, he would never leave.

She needed him to go, even if he didn't want to.

Chapter 5

Carly leaned back against her front door and slid to the ground. After months of forcing her feelings for Anthony deep down inside, she was now screwed.

He'd kissed her.

Oh God, had he kissed her.

She wanted to crawl inside him and never come out. That's how good he'd made her feel. Years of self-doubt and loathing had come crashing to a halt when his mouth had touched hers. After Rob and the scandal with her mom in college, Carly swore that love, and everything that came with it, was not for her.

Until five months ago, when Anthony came into her life.

He was a domineering, cocky, know-it-all.

Except he wasn't. Not really. He was just a guy who was trying to get through life the best way he knew how, the same as everyone else. And in her case, she was not doing it well. At least, not in the guy department.

How she'd ever let that complete douche, Rob, into her heart, she had no clue. If she'd have met him today, without even knowing anything about him, he would not be the type of guy she'd fall for. He was a slick-talking city boy, who gelled his hair back.

Yuck.

Who the fuck gelled their hair? A little paste or pomade was one thing, but all gelled up was gross. When they'd had sex, she made sure she never touched his hair.

Here it was eight years later and she was still letting him dictate her life. She did believe in love; at least the theory of it. And she knew for a fact that what Brandon and Leah, and Logan and Mel had, was real, true, go to the ends of the Earth for each other, love.

That's the kind of love she deserved.

Someday.

Anthony might not be that person – even though it sure felt like he was – but she was no longer going to let what happened in the past dictate her future.

Max came over and sat down next to her, probably starving, since she had been getting ready to feed him when Anthony had knocked.

"You're a good boy, aren't ya, Max." She rubbed his head and scratched his ears. "Let's go get you some food." Standing, she walked to her kitchen, Max hot on her heels. After filling his bowls with food and water, she pulled a frozen dinner from the freezer and popped it in the microwave. Her tea, which she had made when she'd first gotten home from the studio, was already cold from being left undrunk while Anthony had been there. She poured it down the sink and placed the mug in the dishwasher.

When the microwave dinged, she grabbed her food and a fork and walked to the couch. Dinner in front of the TV had become the norm for her since Mel had moved out. When they had both lived there, and then Leah too, they tried to eat together at the table or counter. But since it was just her, she preferred the couch.

She went to grab the remote and instead found her phone. That reminded her that it had been ringing, and she picked it up. There was a missed call from the same number that had been calling for months. She couldn't say why she chose that message to listen to, but she hit play and put the message on speaker.

It was the same message as in the beginning when the attorney had started calling only this time, he sounded desperate. Like extremely desperate. She listened again, to make sure she hadn't missed anything and then deleted it. She didn't want to call him back, but if she was going to put the past behind her, maybe she should.

It couldn't be that bad, right?

Deciding she would make the call in the morning, she went about eating her dinner and watching television. When she finally went to bed and closed her eyes, Anthony's kiss replayed over and over in her mind. She hadn't wanted him to stop. In fact, if he had pushed just a little, they'd probably still be having mind-blowing sex.

She had no doubt a man like him could go for hours and keep her satisfied.

Oh boy, did she need to be satisfied.

Tossing and turning, she groaned in frustration. Why hadn't she just taken what he was offering? Why did she feel the need to think everything through all the time?

That answer was actually pretty simple.

She didn't want to be anything like her mom. Her mom had cheated on her dad multiple times, the last one being with Rob, her own boyfriend. Carly refused to be that way. If she was going to be with someone, then she was only going to be with them. And, they damn well better only be with her.

Anthony's declaration that there had been no one else in all the months since they'd met had melted a small corner of her heart. A heart she had kept carefully guarded. If he could go months without sleeping with someone when she wasn't even his...that had to be good, right?

Turning on her side, she tucked her hands under her face. Did he feel like she did at the thought of dating anyone but him? She'd been able to do nothing but compare guys to him when she had tried to go on dates three months ago. And when she'd made the amazingly awesome decision to try and just have a one night stand, she'd literally gotten sick to her stomach.

She'd known then she was in trouble, no matter how hard she'd tried to deny it.

But now, she was ready. Ready to say fuck it and give it – in this case him – a try.

Stepping out of the studio after her last morning class, Carly, ran smack dab into Mel.

"Hey, how was class?" Carly asked.

"Great. I love teaching those three-year-olds." She and Mel walked down the corridor to where the office was. They hadn't seen each other yet, since Carly had three morning classes and Mel only had the one. They tried to set a schedule which gave them each a couple of mornings a week to sleep in. Same with night classes. They each got one night off.

At the office, they each chatted with a few parents before they left. When the building was silent again, Carly did what she always did after teaching and sat on the floor of their combined office and began to stretch.

"There's something different about you today?" Mel said. "Hey, Leah," Mel shouted. "Does Carly seem different today?"

Carly rolled her eyes as Leah stepped into the office from the lobby. "I haven't seen her yet. What kind of different? Like new hair different?"

"No like, something good happened, different."

"Can you two maybe stop talking about me, and talk to me. I am sitting right here."

"Ya know, now that you mention it, she does seem happier. Not that you aren't always a joy to be around." Leah directed her mocking in Mel's direction.

"Spill," Mel said.

"I feel like I repeat myself a lot with you two, but I really hate you both."

Leah scoffed. "To quote Cher from Clueless, 'as if.'"

Before she could answer, the bell over the front door chimed and a man walked in; a man who looked vaguely familiar to her. He stood at the front desk and Leah got up and walked to the counter to greet him.

"Hi, I'm looking for Carly Graham?" The second Carly heard him speak, she knew instantly why he looked familiar.

He was Rob's brother.

Leah looked back through the doorway at her, and Carly stood up from the floor. She'd never met Rob's brother, but he looked almost identical, and sounded the same.

"I'm Carly," she managed to squeak out when she was face-to-face with him.

"My name is Ryan Ball, you knew my brother Rob. Is there maybe somewhere we could talk in private?" He looked frazzled, even though he was dressed immaculately in a suit and tie.

Carly looked behind her at both Leah and Mel. She didn't know what this was about or what this man had to say, but since Leah and Mel were the only two people in the world who knew the story about Rob and her mom, she wanted them there.

"They are my family. Anything you say, they can hear."

Leah nodded. "Why don't you come on in to the office and have a seat. I'm Leah."

"Ryan." They shook hands and he walked around the counter and into the office.

Thank God for Leah taking charge. Carly was freaked out that Rob's brother was there and her mind wasn't firing on all cylinders. If she remembered correctly, Ryan was a year or two older than Rob, which put him about thirty. And Rob hated him, because he was the golden boy, and could do no wrong.

"I'm Melanie," Mel stood and shook his hand.

Ryan took off his suit jacket and draped it over the back of the chair before sitting. Carly also sat, Leah and Mel flanking each side of her.

"What's this about?" Leah again took the lead, and Carly was grateful.

"There's been an attorney trying to get in touch with you for several months now and you haven't returned his calls."

She nodded and swallowed the lump that had formed in her throat. "I actually decided last night that I was going to call him back."

"I guess this is good timing then." He looked down at his shoes. "I'm not sure how much you know about Rob and your mom's relationship?"

Just hearing the word relationship in reference to her mom and Rob made her cringe. "I don't know anything other than finding them fucking in his dorm Junior year. That was the last contact I had with either of them." She hated to sound crass, but her mom had ruined her life, all because she was a slut.

Ryan nodded. "It was the same for me and my family. My parents were pissed at Rob because, once he hooked up with Tina, his life went in a downward spiral. They did drugs and then he dropped out of school. It was devastating for them. So they did the only thing they could think of and cut him out of their lives."

Carly had never known any of the stories he told, and while she still hated Rob for what he did to her, she was saddened that her mom was the cause of his demise.

"What about you? Do you talk to him?"

He looked ashamed. "I didn't. I was so caught up in my own life that I felt I didn't have time for his crazy ways. We were never close to begin with, so it hadn't been too hard."

"Why are you here now?" Mel asked.

"Six months ago, Rob and Tina got into a car accident." He visibly swallowed and let out a breath. "Rob died instantly."

Shock overtook her body. She'd hated Rob and her mom for what they'd done to her, but that didn't stop her from being sad for a boy she once thought she had feelings for. "I'm so sorry." It was the only thing she could say, there was nothing else.

"What about Tina?" Leah asked, emotion in her voice.

"Tina survived and was in the hospital. But it was bad. She had sustained severe injuries and after three months, she also passed away." His eyes and voice conveyed his grief.

Carly gripped a hand, she wasn't sure if it was Leah or Mel's. All she knew was if she didn't hold onto something or someone she was going to collapse. It didn't matter that she hated her mom. It didn't matter that she'd cheated on her dad and stolen Carly's boyfriend. None of it mattered when she heard the words.

Her mom was dead.

"Oh, God." Breaths were coming fast, and yet, it felt like she couldn't take in air. Gripping her chest she kept trying.

"Put your head down," Leah said and pushed her head down to her knees, "and breathe deep. No short breaths, only deep ones."

A hand was rubbing her back and the room was silent except for her breathing. When she felt she had it under control, she lifted her head.

"I didn't mean to just say it," Ryan said, his hands running back and forth on his legs. "It's just been a crazy few months."

Tears she swore she would never shed over her mom, fell down her cheeks. "Is that why the lawyer has been calling me? To tell me about my mom and Rob?"

"Yes and no." He stood and paced the room, his back to her. When he turned, he said, "They had a child, Tina and Rob."

The whole world came to a crashing halt. She didn't breathe and the tears stopped midstream. It felt like there was nothing but emptiness. She couldn't speak and didn't dare try. Looking to Leah for help, she stepped right in.

"Did the child survive?"

"Oh God yeah, I'm so sorry. I should have said that." He sat back down facing her. "His name is Reed and he is six years old." Carly heard the affection in his voice and his face lit up when he said his name.

"Where is he?" Carly asked, finally able to speak.

"I've been taking care of him since the accident. I was listed as Rob's next of kin and got the call. When I found out Tina's condition was not improving, and most likely wouldn't, I had a decision to make. I could either let Reed go to foster care or I could take him. I had no choice, I had to take him. He's just a kid for christ's sake. He didn't deserve a life in foster care when he had family out in the world. There was no way I could live with myself if I let that happen."

Carly was amazed at how different Ryan and Rob were. Rob wouldn't have thought twice about leaving a kid in foster care. He was only worried about himself.

"Where is Reed now?"

"He's in school for the day, and I have a sitter picking him up and taking him home, until I can get there."

She fidgeted in her chair. "Can I meet him sometime?"

Ryan silently stared at her. "That's actually what I came to talk to you about and why the lawyer was calling you." He stood again. "I need help. I can't do this full time. He's a great kid, but I work sixty hours a week, and I'm never home. He deserves better. More."

Carly's mind swam with all the reasons she couldn't and shouldn't help. The biggest of those being her dad. He had no idea about her mom. After she had caught her with Rob, she gave her mom an ultimatum. Leave and never come back, or else Carly would tell her dad about all the times she had seen her mom with other men. Because she was a coward, and honestly, a shitty mom, she took the deal. Carly hadn't seen her since.

It would break her dad to know all that. To know about the affairs, and the cheating with Rob, and most of all, about the child.

A child, who was pure and good, and didn't deserve any of the bad shit that was happening to him. What kind of person would she be if she didn't help, didn't get to know her own brother?

"I know I have just dropped a bomb in your lap, and I have no right to do so, but Reed, he's such a sweet kid and smart. So damn smart that sometimes I think he doesn't even need me and could raise himself. And then I realize, he probably had, and that just pisses me off."

She no longer had to think. Ryan had been right when he'd said there wasn't a choice. "I'll help." Leah and Melanie had been silent most of the last few minutes. She looked at each of them and said, "I have to."

Mel nodded. "Of course you do. And we'll be here for you with anything you need."

"What do you need from me?" Carly asked Ryan.

"I know it's not easy for kids to go back and forth between two places all the time, but it's the only thing I can think of right now. I just need some time to get my business in order and figure out how to manage a child, and to actually be there for him."

"What if I took him for a month?" Now that she was involved, she moved full speed ahead. "That would give you time to work things out, and then we could work on a schedule of some sort. Maybe come up with a plan?"

"Can you do that, have him for a month? What about your job?"

"Since I own the business, I can work something out." No longer in shock she stood and they began making plans. She would take temporary custody and enroll him in school in Cedarville. During that time, she and Ryan would work out a schedule. He lived in Baltimore, and that would make it hard, but he was willing to do whatever was best for Reed. She could tell from the way Ryan talked about him, he really cared for the boy, and it was breaking his heart to do this. But he wanted to do the right thing, and not seeing him except an hour a day, was not the right thing.

Before he left, they decided he would fly in with Reed on Friday night, and he would stay for the weekend to help get him settled. That gave Carly three days to get her emotions in check and put her house, and life, in order.

The other thing he did before he left was show her a picture of Reed. He was an adorable blue-eyed, blond-haired boy, who looked like a younger version of Rob and Ryan. Seeing it made her all the more sure she was doing the right thing.

When Ryan left the studio, she was exhausted and emotional. It felt as if she had run a marathon, while at the same time arguing for world peace.

"Am I doing the right thing?" she asked out loud to Leah and Melanie.

"No doubt, you are," Leah said. "Will it be hard? Yes. Both physically and emotionally. But you wouldn't be the person I know you to be if you didn't do this."

"Leah's right," Mel said. "As hard as it will be, it would be harder to live with yourself if you stood by and did nothing."

Leaning back in her chair, she closed her eyes.

"How are you doing?" She heard Leah ask. "I mean about your mom?"

Not opening her eyes to look at her friends she said, "I'd written my mom off so many years ago, that other than the brief second when I felt sad, I don't really feel anything." She sat straight again and opened her eyes. "Is that bad?"

"I don't think so," Mel said. "She hasn't been a part of your life for years, and before that, you and she never got along. It's not like you wished her dead. Just because she gave birth to you doesn't make her your mom. Alice has been more your mom since the day you were born."

Carly wanted to think Mel was right, but she still wasn't sure. Was she cold and unemotional if she didn't have any sadness over her mom's death?

"When someone causes you so much pain, you don't need to mourn their loss," Leah added.

Deciding she could stew on it later, she stood up. "I have a couple of hours before my first night class and I think I need to tell my dad before he finds out from anyone else."

"Do you want one of us to go with you?" Mel asked.

"I think I need to do this by myself. I will need to tell Bran and Logan too, along with my aunt and uncle. I might need your moral support for that."

"You got it."

"I'll be back before my class starts at five," she said and left the office. Out in her car, she took several deep breaths to steady herself, before driving away. This was a huge life-changing thing and she needed to make sure she did it all correctly. And that started with telling her dad.

Making a pit stop at her house to grab Max, she saw a truck parked in her driveway.

More specifically Anthony's truck.

She almost backed out without letting him see her only because she wasn't sure she was ready for him right then. She was a wreck and didn't want him to see her that way. But, then she remembered the feeling she felt for a split second when she first saw his truck parked there, and how much joy it gave her.

The calmness he brought when he was just in her vicinity, was enough to make her pull in next to him.

He was sitting in his truck and turned to look at her as soon as she pulled up. Getting out, she crossed in front of his truck and stood by his door. It took him a second, but he rolled the window down.

"What are you doing here?" she asked. His smell assaulted her and she had to reach out and grab the truck to steady herself. Why the fuck did he always smell so good?

"I had to do an update on the system. You should have gotten an email about it a couple days ago?"

She had, but between drunk dialing, kissing and now this thing with Reed, she had forgotten all about it. "I think I remember something about it."

"I didn't expect you to be here."

"I'm running to my dad's to talk to him and I thought I would take Max."

He studied her, his eyes taking in everything. "Is something wrong?" He reached out and brushed his fingers down her cheek making her shiver. "You look...unhappy."

He started to pull his hand back but she grabbed it and held it to her cheek. She had no idea how he was always able to read her, but right then, she didn't care. "I've had a rough day. And, if you have a minute, I think I'd like to tell you about it?" She didn't know what prompted her to say that, or why she even wanted to tell him her story, but again, she wasn't going to question it.

He opened the door and she let go of his hand so he could slide out. They moved to her porch silently, and each took a seat, him on the steps and her on the swing. She had no idea where to begin so just picked the most important thing.

"I just found out I have a six-year-old stepbrother." She let the silence settle over them and waited for his reaction.

"Your dad?"

"No," she corrected, "my mom."

"I thought your mom wasn't in your life?"

She didn't question how he'd known about her mom. "She isn't." She bit her lip and went on. "It's a really long story, part of it is what I alluded to last night that I wanted to tell you. I still want to tell you, but the thing is, I only have a little bit of time and I have to talk to my dad."

"I understand." He nodded once.

"Would you – would you want to come with me?" She cringed. "I understand if you are busy, or if you just don't want to."

"I'll go." His words were strong.

She hadn't planned to ask him, but once she had, it'd seemed right. While Leah or Melanie were the obvious choices, Anthony was the only one who calmed her just by being near. "Thank you." She looked down at her feet and let out a breath she hadn't even been aware she was holding.

These next few hours were going to be difficult for her, even more difficult for her dad. But in the end, she felt she was doing the right thing.

Chapter 6

Anthony had offered to drive to her dad's house and they'd ridden in silence the whole way. When he pulled up and shut off the engine, he turned toward her. "If you decide you don't want me here, I don't have to go inside."

He watched her fidget in her seat and then she started to speak, but stopped. Turning, she looked at him. "This story that I am going to tell my dad, at least the first part of it, is what has shaped my adult life. It's what you need to know in order to understand why I am the way I am. I know I should tell it to you separately and alone but – and please don't think I'm a crazy, insane person for saying this – you somehow make me feel safe and calm."

If he thought she was a crazy person, he'd have to put himself in the same category. "I make you feel safe?" He asked it as a question because he was still in disbelief that she and he were on the same page.

"I know," she rolled her eyes in a classic Carly move, "it makes no sense. But it's the way I feel and you know what? I'm sick of fighting it."

She opened her door and got out, Max anxiously awaiting her to open his door. He jumped out as soon as the door was opened and ran ahead into the back yard. As they walked, he asked, "Does your dad not know this story? I thought you were close?"

"We are," she said, continuing to walk. "This was something I had to do on my own, and I did it to protect him. The only two people in the world I have told this story to are Leah and Mel."

He was shocked again when she didn't mention Logan and Brandon. They were so close, like brothers, that it was hard to believe she hadn't confided in them.

She didn't knock at the front door, just walked in. "Dad, are you here?" He followed her in and shut the door behind them.

Her dad, Mike, walked into the entry and greeted them. Tony had met him twice, both in passing, but he seemed like a good guy.

Reminded him a lot of Logan and Brandon's dad, which made sense, considering they were brothers.

"Hey Carls," he looked at Tony, "It's Tony, right?" They shook hands.

"Yes, sir."

"Come on in." They followed him into the kitchen. "Since I've been around the block a few times, I can only assume you are here with some kind of news?"

"Why don't you sit down, dad?" Carly indicated to a chair at the table.

"Are you getting married?" He looked between the two of them. "Is that what this is about?"

"No, sir." Tony answered with a straight face.

"Dad please, just sit down."

"All right," he said, and sat, both Tony and Carly doing the same.

Tony was chomping at the bit to hear this story that had shaped her life, and to find out the details of this six-year-old brother she'd just found out she had. He couldn't imagine a story that would involve those two things together.

"I have so many things to tell you, dad, and Tony is here because I want him to hear them too, and also, because I need a friend right now." She looked over at him and he nodded. An indication he was ready to hear whatever it was she had to say.

"This is about mom and why she left."

"I don't understand," Mike said. "We know why she left."

"That letter and everything she wrote wasn't entirely true." Carly said. "While she didn't love you anymore, it was more that she loved," she took a deep breath, "other people."

"Carly I don't want to hear any of this," he pushed back his chair and stood. "Why do you want to dredge up the past?"

"Dad, please," she begged. "Just listen."

Mike walked several feet away. "I really don't want to hear this."

"She slept with my boyfriend!" she shouted. "She fucking cheated on you with my boyfriend!"

Tony was thrown, but he stayed quiet. This was her story and she needed to tell it without him interrupting.

Mike turned, his face showing pain. "What are you saying?"

"Junior year, I dated that guy, Rob. One day I walked into his dorm room and he was with another woman. But, not just any woman, it was Mom."

"No," Mike said, and sat back down slowly. "That can't be."

"It's true dad. And what's worse is, that wasn't the first time she had cheated on you." Tony listened intently as she went on to tell him about all the times she had caught her mom leaving the house or coming back home with men. She had just been little, and must have repressed it, because she never remembered it until the night she walked in on her boyfriend.

Tony was in awe of how she told the story without so much as a hint of emotion in her voice. And, yes, it had been years, and she'd had a lot of time to process, but still. It was her mom.

Moms were supposed to protect, not harm.

"Why did you keep this from me for all these years?" her dad asked.

"I didn't want to hurt you." Now there was emotion. Her dad obviously meant a lot to her and, everything she had done, had been for him. He saw a stray tear roll down her cheek, and in an act of comfort, reached for her hand under the table.

"We fought and I gave her an ultimatum. Leave and never come back, or else I would tell you everything I remembered from when I was a kid." She shrugged. "Since she didn't seem to love either one of us, she left."

Tony wanted to do more than hold her hand for comfort. He wanted to find this woman and bash her head in. What woman doesn't love her child?

"Carly," Mike said roughly, and Tony could see the emotion on his face. "I wish you would have told me. You were young and should not have had to deal with any of that." He paused and looked down at the table. "I can't say I'm surprised at her behavior though. She was never a woman who should have been tied down. She hated this town and everything to do with it. She just wasn't cut out for small-town life as a wife and mother."

"Is that why you didn't have more kids? Did she hate me that much?"

"She didn't hate you, she hated being stuck. Having kids meant she had to stay, and that was hard for her. I don't think it helped that from the day she had you, I gave you all the attention and paid very little to her. I think she knew then she could never compete with you."

"Daddy," she said, tears falling faster.

"Maybe it was my fault, maybe I caused this?"

"No," she shook her head. "She was wrong, all you did was love me when she didn't."

A quiet engulfed the room while father and daughter sat and cried together. Tony felt like an outsider, like maybe he shouldn't be watching, but when Carly squeezed his hand under the table, it steadied him.

"There's more."

"I'm not sure if I can handle any more." He gave a small, fake laugh.

"Six months ago, mom and Rob were in a car accident. Rob died on the spot. Mom survived for a few months before dying in the hospital."

"Oh God," her dad said.

"Dad..." she squeezed his hand again. "They had a child."

Mike's face showed shock, and his jaw dropped, but no words came out.

"I just found out this morning. Rob's brother came to see me. He has been taking care of Reed since the accident, but now it's getting harder and he is looking for help. He was trying to do the right thing so Reed wouldn't have to go into the system, but it's just getting too difficult."

"You're going to help?" Mike asked, not accusingly but more of a *you have to* kind of question.

Seemingly shocked, she said, "You don't have a problem with me doing that?"

"Carly, kids should never be held responsible for their parent's actions. You of all people should understand that. He's innocent and he shouldn't pay the price for bad circumstances."

She flew around the table and gripped her dad in a fierce hug. "I'm so glad you think that. I wouldn't be able to live with myself if I did nothing."

"Oh Carls, you're doing the right thing, and even if you weren't, you don't need my approval. You're an adult, and while I might not always agree with your decisions, I have to trust you know what you are doing."

Tony was overwhelmed with how much respect they had for each other. It was so much deeper than just normal father-daughter love. It was mutual, and it was given so freely.

Carly stepped back, glancing at him quickly. "He'll be here Friday, Reed. He and Ryan, Rob's brother, are going to stay with me for the weekend, to get Reed acclimated. After that, Reed will stay for the whole month."

"I'm here to help with anything you need."

She hugged him again. "We better be going. I have so much to do and I still have to work tonight. Is it okay if I leave Max? He loves it here."

"Yep. Leave him as long as you need."

Tony followed her through the house, and after saying goodbye to her dad, walked with her to his truck. On the passenger side of the truck, he opened the door for her and she gave him a strange look before getting in. He didn't question it and went to the driver's side and hopped in.

He started the engine, and just as he was about to put the truck in gear she said, "No one has ever opened a car door for me."

His movements stopped. Had she'd just said what he thought she'd said.

"You're joking, right?"

She shook her head from side to side.

He didn't know what to make of that so he put the truck in gear and backed out. "Well get used to it." He saw her smile out of the corner of his eye. That had been his goal. To give her just a little bit of happiness.

He had been driving for a few minutes when she finally said, "Don't you have anything to say?"

He glanced at her before turning his attention back to the road. "I have a lot to say, but I think it would be better if I waited until I wasn't driving."

"Is it that bad?"

He sighed. She could never just leave well enough alone. "It's not bad at all, it's just that," he looked toward her again, "I'd like to be holding you when I say what I have to say."

"Oh," she said, her lips forming a small O.

He smiled. Keeping her off-balance was one of his great joys in life.

He pulled into her driveway and cut the engine.

"Wanna come in?" she asked. "I still have a little time before I have to be at work."

He answered with a nod, and then followed her up her drive and into her house. She seemed more nervous now than she had at her dad's. He wasn't sure if it was because of what he was going to say, or if she was nervous for him to touch her. Either way, he wasn't going to hold back.

"Come here." He reached for her hand and pulled her backward, spinning her to face him. She went willingly into his arms and he felt her let out a deep exhale once his arms were around her.

For minutes he just held her, stroking her hair and down her back. It felt right, having her in his arms, and if he had the choice, he'd never let go.

But, they needed to talk.

"Let's sit," he said, and backed her up to the couch.

She sat, saying, "I never thought I'd ever have to tell that story again, especially not to my dad."

"There's so much I want to say to you and to tell you, but the one thing that sticks out...that I feel you need to know first, is how fucking in awe of you I am. You had something happen to you that could have made you a cynical, hateful person, and instead, you came out the other side this happy, caring, helpful person. It's remarkable. You're remarkable."

"But I'm not." She scrunched up her face. "I let one shitty experience with a guy I honestly didn't even like that much, and a mom who didn't love me, shape my whole life. He's the reason I don't date, and she's the reason I don't believe in love. How does that make me remarkable?"

He wished she saw herself through his eyes. He saw what she didn't; how incredible it was to come back from something like that.

"It makes you remarkable because here you are talking about it, doing something about it. Not everyone would be able to do that. And taking in a boy, who was your mom's, after what she did to you, Carly, you have to know that very few people on this Earth would do the same. I'm not sure I could."

She reached her hand out and laid it on his thigh. His heart started to beat faster at just her touch. "You could. It's what an honorable man would do."

"Tell me how you're feeling, what's going on inside you?"

She let out a small laugh. "I thought guys didn't like to talk about feelings?"

"You have a lot of years to make up for in learning what guys like and don't like. And while some guys might not want to talk, I do. Especially to you."

"I feel...freaked out. I'm going to be in charge of a kid, who I've never met for a whole month. I like kids, I think. But that's because I teach them for an hour and then send them back home. What do I know about raising a kid?"

"What does anyone know about raising a kid? I have to assume most first time parents go into parenthood a little unsure of how they are going to handle it. You are no different."

"But what if I'm like her?" She said it so low he'd barely heard her. He knew she was talking about her mom and he wished there was some way to promise her that wouldn't happen. But there wasn't.

"Look at me," he said and lifted her chin so she had to look him in the eyes. "I think parenting is a leap of faith. The only things you can do are love and take care and be there for a child. After that, it's not up to us anymore."

She inhaled deeply and closed her eyes. "Why do you always smell so good?"

It was out of the blue and exactly what he'd come to expect from her. "I could ask you the same thing."

"No really." She opened her eyes. "I can't place it but it reminds me of summers when I was a kid."

"Promise not to laugh?" He'd never told anyone this, and it was his one secret.

"Why would I laugh? You just heard my life story and stood by me like a freaking stone statue. I think I can manage not to laugh."

"It's sunscreen. I use it as lotion because it's one of the only things I've found that doesn't make me itch."

"That's it! It's that stuff in the yellow and green bottle."

He nodded and laughed. "Yep."

"It's been driving me crazy for months." She leaned in and sniffed his neck, making his cock go hard. He closed his eyes and breathed deeply, willing it to go down, to no avail. She was practically on top of him as she took in his scent, and he was a goner.

"Carly," he choked out, his voice sounding hoarse and desperate to his own ears.

Just her eyes looked up at him, making him picture her doing the same thing as she sucked his cock.

He was done for.

Gripping the sides of her face, he slammed his mouth to hers with every intention of taking what he wanted and needed from her. But, as soon as her lips touched his, it became more about giving to her and less about taking for himself.

She moaned into his mouth and climbed onto his lap. He had no doubt she could feel his arousal, and it was confirmed when she seated herself more firmly against him.

Desperate for more, he rained kisses over her face until he found her ear. He bit down hard on the lobe, eliciting a loud groan from her.

"Holy shit!" she shouted and grabbed his face in her hands before pulling back to look at him. "I'm thinking I might need to be punished for waiting so long to do this."

If it were possible, his dick grew harder. "I think we can probably arrange that." They kissed again, more desperate and more intense. Her hands moved from his face to his hair, and when she yanked hard on it, he lifted his hips, involuntarily pressing his cock harder into her. She didn't seem to mind though and met him grind for grind.

He wasn't sure how or why, but reality crept in and he remembered, she still had to go to work. And honestly, so did he.

Slowing their kisses he swept the hair from her face and leaned his forehead against hers. "This was probably a bad time to start this."

She smiled and ran a finger across his bottom lip. "See, honorable." She was indicating her words from earlier.

"If it matters, the things I want to do to you are not in the least bit honorable."

She groaned. "Why would you say that? Now all I want to do is find out what they are, and I can't because I have to go to work."

"Soon." He kissed her lightly before they separated. "Can I ask you something?"

"Does it have anything to do with those things you want to do with me?" She gave him a wicked smile and he laughed.

"Stop." He waved her off and got serious. "Do Logan and Bran really not know any of what you told your dad?"

"You just had to go and bring me back to reality didn't you?" She scowled and got up off the couch. "No they don't know, but I need to tell them soon. With Reed coming Friday, I want them to have as much time to process as possible."

Tony stood too and followed her into her kitchen. It seemed he was doing a lot of following her lately, but he didn't care. He'd follow her to hell and back if it meant he got to be with her.

"I think I will try and tell them tonight. That way I don't take the chance of them finding out by accident."

"Probably a good idea. Those two love to gossip." He took the bottle of water she offered him, and twisted off the cap.

Biting her bottom lip, she played with the label on her bottle. He'd seen her do the same thing before, always when she was trying not to say something.

"Say it."

"Huh?"

"Say whatever it is you are trying not to."

"How do you know I want to say something?"

He took two steps toward her and removed the bottle of water from her hand. "You always maul labels when you are trying to keep quiet."

She scowled and grabbed the bottle from his hand. "Well, now I'm not going to ask you."

A laugh escaped him and he leaned the short distance down to be face-to-face with her. "You do know I will give you whatever you want, right? Need me to beat someone up or I don't know, remodel your kitchen? I'll do it. Without hesitation."

She didn't blink or look away. "Now I want to ask what is wrong with my kitchen, but if I do we'll get completely off track, and then I will forget to ask you what I really want to ask you, which is, will you be with me when I talk to Logan and Brandon?"

He tried to hold back his smile, but knew it was an impossible task. "Yes, I'll be with you, and for the record, you can get off task with me whenever you want. I'm starting to enjoy it." Closing the distance between them, he gave her a light, feathered kiss on the lips. "I have to go. I have a meeting at four."

"I have to get to work anyway. I'd like to try to talk to Logan and Brandon tonight. Will you be able to come back here?"

"Text me the details and I'll be there."

He walked out of the kitchen and through the living room, stopping before he opened the front door. "Hey Carly," he said and took a deep breath before looking over his shoulder at her, "I know it seems fast, and a little out of control, and I know your life is about to be turned upside down, but I want to be here for anything you need, anytime you need it."

He didn't wait for her to answer, instead, he just opened the door and walked out.

He didn't know what the future held, but he did know, at least for now, it held her.

Chapter 7

Carly made it to the studio, with twenty minutes to spare, before her first class. Mel was already teaching, but she found Leah sitting at her desk working.

"You look ridiculously happy for someone who got the news you got this morning."

Dropping her bag on her desk, Carly turned to Leah. "My dad was amazing. He supported me, one hundred percent, and said he'd help in any way possible."

"That's awesome. But, for some reason I don't think your dad is the reason for your happy mood."

She smiled and bit the fingernail on her thumb. "Anthony went with me. To tell my dad."

"Seriously?"

"He was at my house when I stopped there and, I don't know, it just felt right to have him with me."

"Did something happen between you two?"

Carly was confused, until she remembered, she had never gotten around to telling Leah and Mel about the kiss she and Anthony had shared the night before. They had been interrupted by Ryan.

Grabbing her chair, she scooted to be right next to Leah. "Monday night, almost right after I got home from here, Anthony showed up at the house."

Eyes wide, Leah whispered, "Oh, this is going to be good."

"He asked, like he had every right in the world to do so, if I was seeing anyone else. Like he and I were seeing each other."

"No comment." Leah imitated zipping her lips.

"I don't have a lot of time before I teach, so stop interrupting me." She knew Leah had opinions on her and Anthony and their 'relationship,' but Carly couldn't worry about that.

"Anyway, I basically chastised him, I don't even remember what I said, but then out of nowhere – and yeah, I know, it wasn't really out of nowhere – he kissed me."

Leah's jaw hit the floor. "Holy mother of baby Jesus. It's about damn time. Tell me about the kiss? Was it hot? It had to be hot. There is no way Tony doesn't kiss hot."

"Would you like to tell the story?" Carly sat back and waved an arm in front of her.

"I think I deserve details for sitting on the sidelines for six months and dealing with all the sexual tension between you guys. So, quit being a stingy bitch, and give them to me."

Carly laughed and sat forward again. "Of course it was hot. Scorching. I was a fucking goner the minute his lips touched mine."

Leah fanned herself and jokingly sang, "Tell me more, tell me more."

Carly heard kids coming down the hall, letting her know Mel's class had ended. She had to hurry. "When he left, he said he wasn't dating anyone else, hadn't wanted to since he met me."

"Ahhh," Leah cooed. "Tony is such a good guy."

Carly stood as students started filing into the lobby. "I'll have to tell you the rest later." She grabbed her bag, but left her purse and phone sitting on her desk and headed to the big studio where her class would start in five minutes. She liked to take time to herself and warm-up before the kids came in, and that day, she needed it more than ever.

She waved to Mel, through the door of the studio across from hers, before stepping into her studio. Mel had another class starting, so there was no time to talk.

As she stretched, she thought back through the last twenty-four hours. The kiss, declaration of not dating anyone, Ryan showing up, finding out her mom was dead, Reed, telling her dad and more kisses with Anthony.

He seemed to bookend her crazy life.

She didn't know where he was going to fit in her life, especially now with Reed, but she knew she wanted him there. It was going to take some figuring out and she was more than ready for the opportunity.

His kisses had opened something in her that had been dormant for too long.

After her two classes were finished, Carly headed back to the office. Mel and Leah were both still there, which was odd, because on Tuesday's Mel was done early and usually went home.

"Hey, what are you still doing here?" She grabbed a bottle of water from their mini-fridge and plopped down on her chair.

"I stayed because Logan texted and said we were all meeting at your house after the studio closes, so it was easier to not go home first."

"Cool. So they must have gotten my message."

"Seems like it." Mel was acting weird and Carly wasn't sure what was up.

"While you were teaching," Leah said, "your phone was dinging every few minutes with texts."

"You could have just turned it off."

"I did. Or I was going to until I saw what the texts were. And who they were from." She was grinning from ear-to-ear like a kid in a toy store.

"Who were they from?" She reached back on her desk and picked up her phone. Swiping it on, she saw she had six messages, five from Anthony. When her eyes skimmed over the top one, she about fell off her chair.

"Holy shit!"

"Now you know why I really stayed," Mel said sarcastically.

Carly stared at her phone and began reading the messages from the beginning.

Anthony:

You say I'm honorable, but is it honorable to want to strip you completely naked out on a boat in the middle of the lake and lick drops of water from your skin.

Anthony:

What about imagining you on your knees on your kitchen floor with my cock filling your mouth. Is that honorable?

Anthony:

Remember the time I walked in on you naked in your bedroom? Since that moment, every day I have imagined doing it again, only this time, I grab you and fuck you up against the wall with the window open so everyone can hear you scream my name.

Carly couldn't stop reading, even knowing Leah and Mel were watching and waiting for a reaction.

Anthony:

You haven't been in my bedroom, but I have this giant bed and the headboard goes up high. High enough for you to hold onto while you sit on my face and I devour you. Not knowing how you taste haunts me. I need to know how you taste.

Anthony:

Am I still honorable? What if I told you the first time I heard those messages you left for me, I jerked off hard and fast. It's all I can do to not, every time I listen to them. I know it's wrong. But I can't delete them. Not until I can get you under me. Maybe not even then.

Carly swallowed and looked up at her friends. They were both smirking at her.

"You've been keeping secrets from us," Mel said. "How dare you."

"Did you guys read these?" She didn't care. They shared everything, even stuff like that.

"If I say no, can I read them again?" Leah ran her tongue over her top teeth. "Ya know, for research."

Carly dropped the phone into her lap. "I'm in serious trouble here guys. What am I gonna do?"

"Cancel this thing with us tonight and drive your ass to Tony's." Mel looked at Leah. "That's what I'd do."

"I can't cancel, I need to tell them about Reed and the sooner the better." She was hot and bothered, and her mind wasn't functioning on all cylinders.

"So Leah filled me in on the kiss last night, but have things progressed far enough for these kinds of texts?"

She sighed. "Did she also tell you he went with me to my dad's?"

"Yeah."

"He sat there the whole time, holding my hand, while I told my dad this secret I had been holding in forever. And he just listened. Even when we got back to my house, he told me how remarkable I was – his words – and how amazing he thought I was. That led to us kissing again only this time with me sitting in his lap. God, I did not want to leave his lap. The man can kiss, and the way he looks at me..." she trailed off and shook her head. "It's intense."

"I'm hot just hearing about it," Leah said. "You guys have been dodging this for so long there is no way it can't be intense."

"Yeah, Addison thinks it's hysterical," Mel added.

"Oh my God! Addison! I was supposed to have lunch with her today."

"Don't worry, we hung out with her and, while we didn't tell her why you weren't there, we made sure she knew it was extremely important."

She dropped her head down and shook it. "My life is blowing up around me and all I can think about is sex with Anthony. What the hell kind of person does that make me?"

"A human one," Mel said. "And, your life isn't blowing up around you. There's just a lot on your plate right now."

"She'd like it if Tony was on her plate." Leah wagged her eyebrows.

"Child," Mel said. "You are a damn child."

"What?" Leah shrugged. "They have been circling around each other for so long, I just can't control my enthusiasm."

"We need to go," Carly said, " but before we do, I need to tell Anthony to meet at my house. How do I do that and not acknowledge his dirty texts?"

"I don't think you can," Mel said.

"Melanie and I will go lock up, and while we do, you text Tony." Both girls stood. "My advice, don't think too hard." They walked out of the office and Carly stared at her phone. Going for broke, and taking Leah's advice, she typed out a message.

Carly:

My house in twenty minutes if you can still make it.

Don't plan on going home after.

She hit send before she had time to change her mind. She wanted him, that went without saying. But, was she ready for everything being with him would entail?

Now that she'd sent the text, she guessed she was going to find out.

Back at her house, she placed an order for pizza, and then opened a bottle of wine.

"Wine?" she asked her friends. The guys weren't there yet, but Leah said Bran had texted saying they were on the way. And she hadn't heard from Anthony since she'd sent the text.

Had he gotten it? Was he just avoiding her? Taking a giant gulp of wine, she tried to relax. Anthony wasn't the only reason her nerves were on edge.

While she hoped Brandon and Logan reacted the same way her dad had when they heard her story, she had no way to know if they actually would. Thankfully, though, she had her dad and Leah and Melanie on her side.

And Anthony.

Taking another sip of her wine, she poured two more glasses and took them into the living room for Leah and Mel.

As they chatted, the door opened and Brandon and Logan walked in, followed by Anthony. Her body went on full alert just looking at him. He zeroed in on her, and the heat that passed between them, forced a shiver to run through her body.

Holy fuck, she was never going to make it through this talk.

"Hey guys," she finally greeted them.

"You better have beer, because I had a shit day," Brandon said.

"When have I ever not had beer?" He passed her and as he did, she slapped him on the arm.

"Bring me one too," Logan said and then looked at Anthony. He nodded and Logan added, "And one for Tony."

After Brandon passed out the beer, he sat next to Leah. "So what's up? Why did you want us all to come over tonight?"

She was sitting on one of her two chairs next to the couch where Leah, Brandon, Logan, and Mel were all sitting. Anthony was standing, but only inches from her, even though there was a chair open next to her. He was like a guard dog, and while it should've driven her crazy, instead she felt secure.

Damn her feelings.

She took her time, telling the story again from the beginning. The guys' would interrupt to ask questions, but other than that, they stayed in control of their emotions. She had Leah and Melanie to thank for that, she was sure. Logan was more silent than Bran, and that shocked her. She had thought he would be the hothead.

Anthony had moved to sit on the arm of her chair, and when she got to the part of the story about Reed, he caressed her shoulder. It kept her calm as she told them all about him and Ryan and what her plan was. As the story came to a close, silence engulfed the room.

"I have a question," Brandon said, breaking the silence.

"Shoot. I'll answer anything I can."

"When did this happen?" He waved his hand in the direction of her and Anthony.

Out of all the things she expected one of them to ask, that was not high on the list. But knowing them, it should have been.

Carly looked up to Anthony taking in his deep brown eyes which held concern for her. "We're in the beginning stages." Anthony smiled at her, bent down, and gave her a chaste kiss. It shocked her a little that he did it at that moment. But only a little. For the most part, she loved it.

"Can I just say, it's about damn time." Brandon stood and walked toward the kitchen, clapping Anthony on the back as he passed. "You two were driving me bat shit crazy."

"Nothing else to say?" she asked, looking at Logan.

He cleared his throat and gave Melanie a sideways glance. "I'm not happy you kept this from us for all these years. We could have been there for you."

Melanie who had been silent the whole time spoke. "She had us. And we always made sure she could talk about it if she wanted to."

"I'm glad she had you." He lifted her hand to his lips and kissed her knuckles. "Still, I'm sorry you had to go through the whole ordeal. And for the record, I think you are doing the right thing helping with Reed. I think everyone in this room feels the same way and would do the same thing if confronted with the situation."

"Thank you, Logan," She stood, going to him and drawing him up and into a hug. "You were always more brother than cousin, but I think you already know that."

Brandon came in with more beer and wine, just as the doorbell rang. "That'll be the pizza," Carly said, reaching for her purse.

"I got it," Anthony said and bypassed her to answer the door.

"Do I get a hug, too?" Brandon asked, holding out his arms. She went into them like she had so many times over the years when he'd been the one to console her.

"Thank you for listening and understanding why I have to do this."

"Anything you need, and I do mean anything, we are all here for you."

She gave him a quick kiss to the cheek before stepping back and heading to the kitchen to help with the pizza. Anthony set them on the counter and turned to her.

"You okay?" He brushed his finger down her cheek.

"I think I'm going to be," she answered honestly, for maybe the first time ever.

Together they got down plates and piled them all with pizza before calling all their friends in to get some. For the next hour, they ate, talked and laughed and she was relieved not to discuss her mom at least for a little while. Starting Friday her life was going to change drastically because of an innocent six-year-old boy who had just lost both his parents. And she was going to need to be there full time.

But for tonight, she could just be herself.

By the time she ushered everyone out the door, she was exhausted. She leaned her back against the front door and closed her eyes. It was hard to believe only a day had passed. Enough had happened in one day to make it feel like a week.

Had it really only been twenty-four hours since Anthony had kissed her for the first time? She touched her fingers to her lips, remembering the feel of his during the kiss.

"Food's all cleaned up," she heard Anthony speak.

Opening her eyes, she took him in. His big frame, clad in jeans and a t-shirt, made the room feel small.

"Thank you."

"I should probably go," he said but didn't move. His eyes were studying her as if trying to read her mind.

"Oh, you don't want to stay?"

He took two steps moving closer to her but then stopped and shook his head. "You've had a pretty insane day. I don't want to add to that."

She smiled and pushed off the door, moving toward him. "That's not what I asked you."

He sighed and she smiled. She loved driving him crazy. "Of course I want to stay. But it doesn't matter what I want, it only matters what you want."

She raised her eyebrows. "It only matters what I want? Really? So, if I want you to strip naked right here, right now, you'd do it?" His expression changed from concerned to feral. Her body went on high alert just looking at him.

"Is that what you want?" His voice had changed. It was lower, more seductive now.

She hesitantly ran her tongue over her top teeth. He was giving her an out. She could say the word and he would go home, giving her more time to think about what she wanted. Or, she could take what she knew she wanted and have the sexiest man she had ever laid eyes on, in her bed. Naked. Doing very wicked things to her.

Yeah, it wasn't even a contest.

"Yes." Her voice was strong and held not a hint of insecurity.

She wasn't sure who moved first and didn't really care. He was in her arms, kissing her, and that was all that mattered. She wanted him with a need that was so strong, it scared her.

His arms were strong around her waist and she let herself relax knowing he had her.

"Those messages earlier," he said as he kissed her neck, "were they too much too soon?"

Gripping his hair, she pulled his head back to look at him. "You're kidding right? They had me so hot, had I been home alone, I would have pulled my vibrator out and read them over and over as I made myself come."

He groaned and took her lips again, this time backing her up and through the room. "Bedroom," he said against her mouth.

She didn't want to let go of him but had no choice if she wanted to make it upstairs in one piece. "Let me just lock up." She was surprised she could think straight when heat was pouring out of her body. Somehow though, she managed to quickly lock the doors and turn off all the lights. Anthony was waiting at the bottom of the steps and he took her hand as they ascended to her room. It surprised her that she wasn't at all nervous. If anything she was frantic to be with him.

Sitting on the bottom of her bed still holding onto Anthony's hand she looked up at him. "Are you gonna strip now?"

He let out a small laugh. "Are you?"

"If I recall this is my show and I want you naked. Now."

The heat, which had never really left his eyes, was now radiating out of him. Dropping her hand, he grabbed his t-shirt from the neck and pulled it over his head.

How the fuck did guys do that, and why was it so sexy?

His bare chest was all she could stare at, but she heard him kick his shoes off and then his fingers were at the snap of his jeans. She was hypnotized as he unsnapped them and lowered the zipper. She could see a hint of navy underneath, and as he began to push the jeans down his legs she saw that it was boxers, not briefs, he wore. And, under those briefs was an impressive erection.

Needing contact with him more than she could ever remember needing anything, she reached out and touched his abs. His intake of breath told her he was as affected by her touch as she was by touching him.

"Your turn," he said gruffly.

Smiling, she stood, her hand never leaving his skin. "I was thinking maybe you would like to do it." Tilting her head to the side she looked up at him through her lashes.

He leaned in, letting her feel his hot breath on her face. "If I do it, you won't get the chance to wear this ever again."

She shivered at his meaning. He was going to rip her clothes off her. Holy hell. Had anything turned her on more?

"I never liked this shirt anyway."

His nostrils flared and his hands gripped the neck of her tee. When she heard the sound of material ripping, she was a goner. She wasted no time in helping him by pushing her tights down her legs leaving her in only a sports bra and underwear.

She was just about to grab him, when he took a step backward.

"You are fucking gorgeous." She'd read enough romance novels in her life to assume the expression on his face was the same one the male always used when looking at the woman he desired.

She'd never wanted that serious, all-consuming expression directed toward her. She had been fine only reading about it.

She had been wrong. Severely wrong.

Having a man look at you, with all that heat and genuine honesty, was better than the best sex she could imagine.

It would almost be enough.

Almost.

She swallowed and reached out to him. "Please don't make me wait anymore." Her voice sounded foreign to her. Who was this woman inside her who had taken over her body and demanded Anthony was the only one who could give her what she needed?

And why was she so willing to just let it happen?

Chapter 8

Standing in front of a mostly naked Carly, was Tony's version of heaven. She was beautiful. So beautiful he was finding it hard to move. But when she asked, in a voice that was desperate and needy, for him not to make her wait, he was like a rocket. His body moved forward as his arms wrapped around her. He continued moving until they both fell to the bed, him on top of her. He tried to keep his weight from crushing her, but she just kept pulling him closer. Frantic kisses turned to deep sensual ones as they gained composure and found their rhythm.

He needed more of her, all of her really, and couldn't wait another minute. Kissing down her neck, his fingers found their way to her sports bra. Along with Carly's help, he pushed it up and over her head leaving her magnificent breasts on display. He'd seen them that day, almost six months ago, when he'd accidentally walked in on her naked. And since that moment, they were all he thought of. Perfect and pink, they were small but plenty enough for him. His fingers were just about to touch one perfect nipple when Carly's voice stopped him cold.

"I know they're small." Her voice was barely a whisper, but he heard her uncertainty.

Feathering his fingers lightly on the underside of each breast he tilted his head. "I happen to love small."

"You don't have to say that."

"Look at me," he told her as his fingers continued teasing her skin. "It's you and me here in this bed. No one else. When I tell you your tits are awesome, I'm gonna need you to believe me."

"No one has ever thought they were awesome before. The exact opposite usually."

"Those guys were fucking idiots." He punctuated his remark by tweaking one nipple between his finger and thumb.

"Holy shit." She arched her back off the bed.

"Liked that, did you?" He did it again, this time to the other nipple.

She moaned and that was all the encouragement he needed. His guess was that if other guys had told her she was lacking, they hadn't spent enough time paying attention to the way she reacted to her nipples being played with.

He was overjoyed to be her teacher.

Ready for more and to show her just how much he loved her breasts, he lowered his mouth and took one into his mouth. She squirmed under him murmuring incoherent words and gripping his hair tight. He tortured each nipple several times, with both his mouth and his fingers, before continuing his path down her body.

"Mother of God," she huffed out. "'How did I not know?"

Against her skin he laughed. "You just needed me to show you." She laughed and he kissed her stomach. When he reached her underwear he looked up with his eyes to make sure she was still game for what he was about to do.

Her eyes were trained on him and she kept them there as he lowered her underwear. She helped by kicking them off once they were halfway down. He moved the rest of the way down her body until his shoulders were between her thighs. Dropping his gaze from her face, he took in the view in front of him. He was floored to find her pussy bare and glistening with her moisture. Using just a finger he dipped it inside her wetness and drew it down.

"Oh, God."

His cock throbbed with need, but first before he could please himself, he had to taste her. The only problem was, once he put his tongue on her, he might never come up for air.

"Anthony, please," She begged him, and being the gentleman he was, he gave her what she wanted.

The first taste of her sent him over the edge. He'd wanted to go slow, savor the experience. But he was dead in the water once his tongue got a taste. He licked and ate at her with total abandonment. And when it wasn't enough, when he knew she needed more, he added a finger.

Pumping his finger in and out, he sucked her clit into his mouth, until he felt her tense against his tongue.

"Fuck, fuck, fuck! Oh God, fuck!" She pulled at his hair as she came and he had no choice but to let up and just watch. Her eyes were closed and her mouth was open. Her body was bright red, almost as if the whole thing was blushing.

It was sexy as fuck.

He slipped from the bed, picking up his jeans to grab his wallet. He wasn't in the habit of carrying condoms with him everywhere he went, but tonight after she had texted, he'd slipped a couple in, just in case.

"Where'd you go," she asked when he rejoined her.

"Condom." He rolled it down his length as she watched. He was harder than he had ever been and knew this first time was going to be fast.

"I apologize now for how short this is going to be." He lined himself up and began sliding inside.

"I don't care. I just want you inside me." She threaded her arms around his back and forced him deeper. It was too much too soon. He had to force himself to hold back as long as possible. He pushed the last little bit in and instead of just enjoying the feel, he began pumping away. The way she was grinding against him and holding on, let him know she didn't care.

They seemed to want the same thing, and that was each other.

Ducking his head, he took one of her nipples into his mouth and sucked and teased it as he continued to pump in and out. He wasn't going to last long, it felt too fucking amazing, but there was no way he was going before she came again.

Slowing up just a little, he gave deep, long strokes, practically pulling all the way out each time. Her breathing quickened and with one last thrust, and tweak of her nipple, she came, shouting out as she did so.

He was right behind her, holding himself against her as the last amounts of his release drained from his cock.

He'd been dreaming of this day for months, but his dreams didn't hold a candle to the real Carly.

"I'm an idiot," she said, making him lift his head to meet her gaze. "Why didn't you push harder all those months? I gave up six months of awesomeness because I was an idiot."

Rolling to the side, he pulled out of her. "I was as much of an idiot as you were." Removing the condom, he stood. "Be right back." She didn't have a bathroom in her bedroom, so he had to go out into the hallway to throw the condom away.

When he returned he found her in the same position, not having moved a muscle. He was mesmerized by her beauty and just stood in the doorway looking at her.

"I know you're there. Stop staring at me."

He laughed. "How do you know I'm staring at you?" He moved back to the bed.

She rolled to her side and propped her head up onto her hand. "It's a feeling I get. I know without looking when you walk into a room."

This surprised him. "Really?"

"It's annoying and I hate it, so don't make a thing out of it."

He nodded and tried not to laugh. Of course she would hate being aware of him.

"Remember the night I tried to kiss you and I asked you for more?"

Remember? He'd never forgotten that night. It was one that haunted him every day. She had offered herself to him, and he'd said no because she was drunk. After that, he'd been so afraid she'd never want him again. "Yeah," he said cautiously, having no idea where she was going with this.

"I'm really glad you turned me down." That was not what he had expected her to say. "If we'd had sex that night, it wouldn't have been like what we just did. So thank you."

He cupped her face. "You're welcome." He leaned down and kissed her. He'd meant it to be a sweet, quick kiss, but she deepened it, making his cock hard again.

She rolled on top of him, her naked body covering his. He loved the feel of her skin against his and wondered how he'd ever lived without it.

They made love again, and then one more time, before they both fell into an exhausted sleep. He wasn't sure what tomorrow would bring, but he hoped it was more of the same.

When he opened his eyes the next morning, he was disoriented, until he looked down and saw Carly wrapped around him. Like, physically wrapped around him. Her legs were thrown over his, her head rested on his chest, and her arm was tucked under his back.

Had they slept this way all night? Not that he minded. He'd take her any way he could get her, even if it was only in her sleep. It just seemed out of character for her. He had no idea how she liked to sleep, but he imagined it wasn't like this. She was too independent to need anyone, even in her sleep.

"You're doing it again," she said sleepily, her voice vibrating against his chest.

"What am I doing?" He stroked her hair with his free hand.

"Staring at me." She tilted her face up to look at him.

"You might have to get used to that. I like looking at you."

She sighed and rolled her eyes. But, what she didn't do is say anything else, and that was a win in his mind.

He glanced at the clock and noticed it was after eight, and while he'd much rather stay in bed with Carly all day, he had to work. "I'd better get up."

"I know, me too." Neither of them moved though. They stayed wrapped up in each for a few more minutes.

Resigned, she said, "I really do have to get up now," and sat up.

"Why don't you go shower and I will bring you some coffee?" He could use a shower too, but if it was a choice between a shower and smelling like Carly all day, he'd take the latter.

In the kitchen, he found her coffee pot and got busy making the coffee. He knew she liked it strong, so that's what he did. He also knew she liked just a little bit of creamer, so he fetched the bottle from the fridge. When the coffee was finished, he poured two cups, added the creamer, and went back upstairs.

He found her already getting dressed and was a little sad. Seeing her naked one more time would have been a better wake-up than the coffee.

"Here ya go." He held her coffee out to her and she took it.

"Thanks." She took a sip and set it down on the dresser before sitting to put on socks and shoes. "I have no idea how I'm going to get everything done that I need to get done before Ryan and Reed show up on Friday. I mean, what does he even eat? Does he need clothes?"

"Hey, hey, settle down. There are a lot of people who are willing to help you. Me included."

She dropped her foot and sighed. "I know, but tell me the truth. Am I getting in over my head here?"

He knelt in front of her. "No. You're doing something amazing for a kid who deserves a chance at a good life."

She reached out and touched his face. "I wish I saw myself the way you see me. I'm pretty awesome, it seems."

He turned his face in her hand and kissed her palm. "I think so."

"All right," she stood up, "I can do this. I'll go to work, shop during my break, and then work again tonight."

He stood with her. "I need to wash up a little before I leave, are you going to be here a little longer?"

"I have about twenty minutes before I have to leave."

"I'll be done by then." He took his coffee and went to the bathroom to brush his teeth. He wanted this every day, to be with her, but he knew her life was in upheaval and had no idea where he fit into that life. He was afraid, if he asked, he'd scare her off. He made a pact with himself to keep quiet and just let things play out.

He just hoped he could follow through with it.

He found her downstairs, making a to-go cup of coffee.

"I'm all done and should head out." He had a meeting at nine and he still had to drive to the office. He didn't walk into the kitchen but stayed in the living room.

"Hey, Anthony." She looked up at him. "I don't know what I'm doing or what's going to happen, but I have to put Reed first."

He dropped his bag and walked into the kitchen. "Just do me a favor, don't push me out."

"I think that's going to be impossible after last night."

"I know we started this at the worst possible time, but I meant it when I said I would be here to help. With anything. And I don't just mean sex. If you need anything, you can call me."

She smiled. "And if what I need is sex?"

"Definitely call me for that." He bent and brushed his lips across hers. "I really gotta go or my boss might fire me."

"You're the boss."

"Yeah, and I can be a real jackass."

She smirked. "I know."

He walked away from her smiling. "I'll text you later," he said, and opened the front door.

"The same kind of texts you sent me last night?"

He turned his head. "You'll just have to wait and see."

Chapter 9

Carly should have been tired, after all she and Anthony had been up half the night having sex. That, on top of her stressful day, would normally be enough to put her in a coma. But, for some reason, she was energized and she couldn't stop smiling.

That was all Anthony.

He'd been amazing. And the things he'd done to her and made her feel…holy guacamole. It had been fantastic. Beyond anything she'd ever had or even imagined. She wasn't a shy person and had never been timid in bed, but Anthony was on a whole new level. The amount of time he'd spent on her breasts had shocked her. Every guy she had ever been with always stayed away from them and she'd assumed it was because they were small. But Anthony, he seemed to actually like them. And, she'd more than liked how it felt to have his mouth on them.

She walked into the studio to a lobby full of parents and kids waiting for classes to start. Leah was helping a parent and Melanie was at her desk drinking coffee.

"It's about time you got here. I need details."

Carly looked out to the lobby. "This probably isn't the right time or place."

She motioned Carly closer. "Just tell me, was it awesome?"

Carly laughed and shook her head. "Awesome doesn't even begin to describe it."

Mel sat back and smiled. "Later, I want many, many details."

"Later I will be busy buying all the things I need to take care of a six-year-old." Together they stood, left the office and walked toward their studios.

"Since Leah and I plan on helping you, you'll have plenty of time to tell us." She entered her favorite studio and waved over her head to Carly.

Carly spent the next two hours teaching kids how to do ballet and tap. When the last of the parents and students had left the building, she finally sat down in exhaustion. It seemed her late night and crazy day had finally caught up to her.

"I'm wiped."

"I'm actually surprised you're here today," Leah said. "Mel and I were totally prepared to cover for you."

"I wouldn't do that to you guys. Plus, I needed normal, and teaching is what I'm used to."

"You ready to get out of here and shop?" Mel was standing next to her.

"You guys don't have to waste your free time helping me."

Melanie pulled her up out of the chair. "Seriously, this is what we do. Friends help friends, and right now, you need our help."

"Mel's right," Leah said. "Now let's go get some awesome stuff for this little boy."

They spent hours going from store to store getting all kinds of things. She got bedding she thought a six-year-old might like, a bunch of different toys and books. She even texted Ryan to find out what size clothes he wore and then bought him several outfits. She wanted him to have everything he needed to be comfortable in her home.

Their last stop was the grocery store. Ryan had also told him some of his favorite foods and she wanted them stocked in her house.

The three of them strolled through the store grabbing anything they thought she'd need.

"When are you going to see Tony again?" Leah added several boxes of cereal to the cart.

"We didn't really set a time. He said he'd text me."

"Let me rephrase," Leah said. "When do you want to see Tony again?"

Carly laughed. "Five minutes after he left my house."

"Good sex will do that to a person," Mel said.

"Shhh," Carly said. "You can't shout the word sex in the grocery store."

"Pfft, that's a stupid rule. If you can have sex in a grocery store you can totally say the word."

"When have you had sex in a grocery store?" Carly whispered.

Melanie looked side-to-side, making sure no one was near them. "Last week."

"No way!" Leah practically shouted. "That did not happen."

"Well, we weren't in the middle of the store but we were in the backroom."

Carly looked at Leah and they wore matching 'Are you fucking kidding me' faces.

"I'm not sure whether to be shocked or high five you. When did you get so daring?"

"It's Logan. That man can get me to do anything. Even have sex in the backroom of a grocery store."

"Damn," Leah swore. "Bran is gonna have to up his game."

Carly covered her ears. "This is grossing me out. These guys are my cousins."

"But friend trumps cousin, in this situation, so you are forced to listen." Mel, always with her reasoning.

"Ya know, making up rules as we go along, doesn't mean we have to follow them?"

Leah broke up their bickering. "Can we get back to the original topic here? When are you going to see Tony again?"

"I was thinking about seeing if he wanted to come by again tonight."

"That means you like him then, right?" Leah was always fishing.

She sighed. "Of course I like him, we've already gone over that. But liking him doesn't mean I have any clue what I'm going to do with him. The man sets my insides on fire with just a look. How am I supposed to deal with those feelings and the fact that come Friday, I'm going to have a six-year-old living with me?"

"Lots of sex in hidden places?" Leah suggested. "I'm sure Melanie over here could give you some ideas?"

The three of them stood in the middle of the canned goods aisle at the grocery store laughing and laughing. It felt good to be able to laugh after all that was going on. She was afraid after Friday, she might never laugh again.

After she dropped off all the stuff she'd purchased that day, she drove back to the studio for her night classes. She had three and wouldn't be finished until after eight. Sitting in her car once she pulled up to the studio, she grabbed her phone. As much as she wanted to see Anthony after her classes, she wasn't sure it was a great idea. She needed sleep and to start getting things organized for Reed. And that meant not seeing Anthony.

She had just swiped her phone on when she saw she had a text. Opening the messages, she found it was from Anthony over an hour ago.

Anthony:

I hope you are having a great day. It's been hell walking around all day smelling like you. I was a masochist to think I could survive the day like this.

She laughed a little, out loud. That's what he did to her. Made her laugh. And, she was beginning to realize, she hadn't done enough of that in the last few years.

Instead of thinking, she answered with the first thing that came to her.

Carly:

You might have had a hard time smelling like me but I had an even harder time not being able to smell you. What I wouldn't give to rub your body all over mine.

She hit send before she could change her mind. His reply was instant.

Anthony:

What time do you get off?

She should say no. Stick to her guns and try to get some sleep. But her fingers had other ideas.

Carly:

8:00. Meet me at my house. Shower first, so I can smell you and not myself.

She was blown away by how easy it was to say things like that to him. Her inhibitions had always been low, but with Anthony they were at a whole new level altogether.

She had known that as soon as she gave in and touched him, she was going to be a goner. The attraction was so strong and she had no power against it. Not that she wanted to. At least not anymore.

Stepping out of her car, she headed into work knowing she only had four hours until she got to see Anthony again.

Four long hours.

When her last class ended she practically ran out of the building. She wanted to shower before Anthony showed up, plus she was starving. There was leftover pizza, so the food part was covered. In her driveway, she sprinted from her car, and ran straight upstairs and into her bathroom. She'd left the front door unlocked just in case Anthony showed up before she was finished.

After a quick shower, she walked out into the hallway before stepping into her room with a towel wrapped around her waist. She flipped on her light and there, on her bed, legs crossed out in front of him was Anthony. She didn't even flinch at his presence. Somewhere, deep inside her body, she had known he would be there.

They didn't speak, and she moved to her dresser and pulled out cotton shorts and a t-shirt all while he watched her. Dropping the towel, she had the pleasure of watching his eyes go wide and feral at her naked body.

Then she pulled the shorts on and he practically choked. "No underwear?"

"I figured, why dirty a pair when I don't plan on wearing them that long." Her goal had been to turn him on with what she was doing, but watching his reaction was making her hot. So hot, she was thinking of skipping dinner and going straight to dessert.

As if he read her mind, he said, "If I didn't know how hungry you were, I'd have your ass on this bed so fast."

Slipping the t-shirt over her head she looked at him. "I'm pretty sure I can eat fast."

He jumped off the bed and followed her downstairs. "I'm gonna heat up some of the leftover pizza, do you want some?"

"I wouldn't say no." While she did that, he grabbed a beer. "What are you drinking?"

"Just water, please." He got her a bottle of water and set it on the counter. "How was your day?" she asked.

"Busy. I had an install and then a couple of service calls. What about you?"

The microwave dinged and she pulled a plate out from inside. "Same. After our morning classes, Leah, Mel and I went shopping." She indicated all the bags in her living room. "As you can see, we bought out the stores."

"I see that. Are there things you still need to get?"

She handed him a plate and then sat down on the stool next to him. "I don't think so. The only thing I was unsure of was a car seat but Ryan said he would just leave his for me to use. So for now, I think I have everything covered."

"What about school?"

"I called about enrolling him and they said once he's here, I can bring him and all the paperwork to get him set up."

"Seems like you have everything covered."

"There is one problem." Earlier when she had called Ryan, he had mentioned Reed was afraid of dogs. Which meant she'd have to have Max stay with her dad full time, or at least until Reed became comfortable.

"What's that?" he asked around a bite of pizza.

"Max is going to have to continue to stay with my dad because it seems Reed is afraid of dogs."

"Does your dad mind?"

"Not at all. He loves Max and when I asked him earlier, he said it wasn't an issue. It'll just be weird not having him here."

"I think you'll be pretty busy."

She swallowed a bite of pizza. "You're probably right."

When they were both finished eating, they cleaned up, and as they were doing so, she yawned.

"You're tired, I should just go home."

She turned to look at him. "Are we really going to do this again? I wouldn't have told you to come over if I didn't want you here."

He looked like he had more to say, and she didn't want to hear it. What she wanted was to do one of the things in his text messages from the other day. Taking two steps toward him, she stood on her toes and kissed him. She felt him relax under her touch and he deepened the kiss. As they kissed, she moved her hands between them and started to unbutton his jeans. She lowered the zipper and then pushed the jeans down over his hips. Breaking their kiss, she began to lower herself to the floor, never taking her eyes off of his.

"Carly," he whispered.

She pulled his pants the rest of the way down his legs, taking his boxers with them. His cock sprang free and she sat back on her heels to admire it.

"You know I'm dying here, right?" he said from above her.

Reaching out, she cupped his balls in her hand. "Then I guess you'll die a happy man." Leaning forward, she slid her tongue up the underside, from base to tip. She heard his groan and did it again loving the feel of him on her tongue. This time when she got to the top she engulfed him in her mouth and sucked hard.

"Mother fucker!"

His cursing and obvious enjoyment spurred her on more. Taking him deeper each time, she used her tongue and even grazed his skin with her teeth. He seemed to like it so she did it several more times.

"Carly, stop. You have to stop."

But she didn't. She kept going ,pleasing himself and her. She'd been dreaming of doing this for months, and now that she had him in her mouth, there was no way she was stopping until he came. She didn't have to wait long. His hands gripped her head gently, as he exploded in her mouth. She swallowed every drop before loosening her mouth on him and sitting back.

Looking up, she saw his eyes glued to her as he gasped for breath. He looked like a strong wind could knock him over and it was hot to know that she was the cause.

"You okay up there?" She bit her bottom lip and tilted her head.

"Holy fuck," He kicked his jeans off the rest of the way before kneeling on the floor in front of her. Taking her face in his hands, he kissed her. "You continue to surprise me."

"It was your idea."

"But, your follow-through was spot on."

She laughed and wondered why she never knew relationships could be sexy, but also fun. She had a lot to learn.

By Friday, she was nervous as hell. She'd done everything she could to prepare for Reed to stay with her. He and Ryan were due to arrive at her house any minute and she spent that time pacing back and forth. Everyone, including Anthony, had volunteered to be there with her, but she felt it best if it was just her. Reed already had a lot to deal with and adding a bunch more people probably wasn't wise.

She'd seen Anthony again the previous night and they'd once again gone at it like bunnies. From her knowledge which was admittedly limited, guys had always been one and done. But not Anthony. That man had the stamina to rival a marathon runner. Not that she was complaining. The more he could go, the more orgasms she had, and there was nothing bad about orgasms.

It wasn't all sex though. They talked and laughed about all kinds of things. And he got her. Like really got her. If she told a story, he could predict how she would react before she told it. She kept joking that he was psychic.

She heard a car pull up and looked out the front window. She saw Ryan exit the vehicle and move to open the rear door. Taking a final deep breath, she opened her front door and walked onto her porch.

Lifting her hand in the air, she greeted them. "Hey, Ryan."

"Hi, Carly." An adorable brown-haired boy stepped from the car and stood next to him. She stepped off her porch and moved toward them.

"You must be Reed?" she asked and squatted to be eye level with him. "I'm Carly." She held out her hand.

"Mmhmm," he nodded and tentatively shook her hand. "Uncle Ryan says you are my sister." He looked up at Ryan as he asked his question. His voice was clear and concise and he didn't seem at all shy. She taught a lot of six-year-olds and you never knew what you were going to get.

"I am your sister. Is that cool or weird?" she said in her kid-friendly voice that she used daily to teach.

He shrugged. "Can it be both?"

Carly laughed. "Absolutely." She stood. "Why don't you guys come on in? I baked some cookies and I could really use someone to help me eat them."

"I like cookies," Reed said walking next to her. "My favorite is chocolate chip."

"Ahh," she exaggerated and put her hand to her chest. "Mine too." She directed him to the table where he sat and ate a cookie. She stood back with Ryan and watched.

"You're already good with him. I don't think you are going to have any problems."

"Being nice is easy, it's when I have to be a disciplinarian that I worry I'll fail."

"If he's anything like he has been with me, you won't have to discipline him. He seems to know right from wrong almost as if he's afraid to make a mistake. If I had to guess, he learned because he got yelled at often if he did something wrong or bad."

Damn her mom and Rob. No kid deserved to grow up that way, especially not one as sweet as Reed. But, that was going to change.

"I set you up in my spare room upstairs and Reed has his own room next door."

"I really appreciate this, thank you. I brought all the guardianship paperwork. You just have to sign it, then we can get it notarized and mailed. My lawyer said we shouldn't have any problems."

She was relieved, because the last thing Reed needed was more upheaval. "Reed, would you like something to drink?"

He shrugged. "I don't need anything." The way he said it told her he didn't want to put her out, not that he didn't want anything. She sat down next to him at the table. "I have a whole fridge full of all kinds of things to drink. Water, milk, juice and there's no way I can drink it all myself. You'd really be helping me out if you drank something."

His eyes lit up like it was the Fourth of July. "I really like chocolate milk. Do you have any of that?"

"Why don't you go check." He jumped up from the table and ran around the corner to the kitchen. She watched as he opened the door and spotted individual cartons of chocolate milk.

"You do have it!" He held one up.

Carly smiled and looked back at Ryan. He was also smiling. "Now you see why I had to take him."

She spent the next several hours settling Reed into the house. She made sure he knew where the bathrooms were, and anything he might need in the kitchen. When he saw his room for the first time she was a little disappointed he wasn't more excited, but then again, she really didn't know what six-year-olds liked.

She made hamburgers for dinner since Ryan had previously mentioned Reed enjoyed them, and then together, they put him to bed. Ryan also disappeared to his room, claiming he had work to do.

Alone she picked up her phone and texted Leah and Melanie.

Carly:

He's freaking adorable.

Melanie:

Of course he is. He's related to you.

Leah:

I can't wait to meet him.

Carly:

I'm thinking of bringing him by the studio tomorrow after classes are over. Maybe you guys could stay and meet him then?

She had taken the day off so she had time to spend with Reed and let him get to know where he would be living. The studio was a good place to start since he would be spending some time there.

Leah:

Of course we'll stay.

Melanie:

Count me in.

That settled, she turned on the TV. Only nothing was keeping her attention. She was restless and she knew what the problem was.

Anthony.

She hadn't seen or talked to him since he'd left her house that morning and she was starting to have withdrawal. Like bad.

And honestly, that kinda pissed her off.

She hated needing people, but worse, she hated wanting them. What the hell had she gotten herself into?

Still it didn't seem to matter, she wanted to talk to him.

Carly:

Hey...

She knew it was lame as soon as she hit send. What she'd really wanted to say – come over and fuck me – she couldn't say because she had a six-year-old in the bedroom next to her.

Anthony:

I was waiting to hear from you. How's it going?

Carly:

Not horrible. He is a freaking adorable kid and so sweet.

Anthony:

That's good. Is he sleeping?

Carly:

Yeah, for about 20 minutes.

Anthony:

What about Ryan:

Carly:

In his room working.

Anthony:

This is gonna make me sound like a jealous ass but I hate the thought of him alone with you in your house.

She re-read his text. It did make him sound jealous, but funnily, she liked it. A lot. What the fuck did that say about her, that she liked when a guy was jealous for no reason at all?

Carly:

First, we aren't alone. Second, eww, yuck. And third, haven't we already discussed that, for some unfathomable reason, you are the only guy I want?

Anthony:

You can't say things like that to me when I'm not there to kiss you. Man, I miss kissing you.

Carly:

You just kissed me this morning. If my memory is correct, I believe you kissed me in several places.

Anthony:

You're the devil.

Carly:

If you didn't live so far away, I'd tell you to come by for a 5-minute kiss. Anywhere on my body you want.

Anthony:

What if I told you I was at Logan's?

Carly:

I'd say "Thank the fucking lord."

Anthony:

5 minutes.

She hit the bathroom quickly and then went out on her porch. She didn't want to wake Reed and didn't want him to walk in on her and Anthony making out. The porch was a safe place.

She sat on her swing and waited for him to drive up. When he finally did, her heart was beating a mile a minute. He stepped out of his truck, looking better than any man had the right to look. Long legs covered in jeans and a navy collared shirt with his logo on the chest. The man was a walking sex symbol. And, he was all hers.

"Are you hiding from me over there in the corner?" he said as he climbed on the porch.

"Just waiting for a hot guy who is on his way over to kiss me."

"Yeah? Will any hot guy do or does it have to be a certain one?"

He was standing above her, looking down. She wanted to climb his body and devour him. But she held strong.

"It has to be a certain one. Maybe you know him. He's tall, built, and looks at me like I hold the answers to every question ever asked."

His nostrils flared, and in an instant, he'd pulled her up and into his arms. She went willingly, because his arms were the only place she wanted to be.

They never went further than kissing, both of them knowing she only had a few moments to spare. She wished it was more, wished she could invite him in and snuggle up next to him in her bed. Sleeping alone, after three nights of having Anthony in her bed was not going to be easy.

There were going to be a lot of lonely nights in her future.

Chapter 10

Anthony was losing his fucking mind. It had been two days since he'd seen Carly and he was about to combust. And, not just from sexual frustration, although that was at least fifty percent of the cause. It was more than that. He missed her. Missed her funny comments and run-on sentences. Missed how she rolled her eyes, and how she always, always, had a witty comeback.

He'd missed her so much that he'd driven into Cedarville both Saturday and Sunday in the hopes that he'd maybe catch a glimpse of her. He knew that was stalking, and had even tried to come up with other reasons to be in town, just in case he ran into her. It hadn't mattered though because he never saw her.

He'd been relegated to going home and clicking through all her pictures on Facebook.

He was a sick bastard.

She texted him both days, but only quick hellos, because she was busy. He understood. Really he did. It just sucked. They'd just gotten started in whatever this relationship was and now they had to spend a lot of time apart.

He knew she had taken the whole week off of work to help Reed get settled. Since Ryan had left Sunday night, she was alone trying to figure everything out. He wanted to help and wished she would ask him, but he didn't want to intervene or step on her toes.

He had just entered his office and found Addie sitting at her desk already. Normally he was the first one there.

"You're early today?"

"McKee is coming in early." John McKee was a new client and Addie had been taking care of the account.

"Are you good or do you need me?"

"I got it. It's fairly straightforward."

He headed into his office and sat down. Since he'd had nothing to do over the weekend, he'd spent most of it catching up on work. That meant he now had virtually nothing to do. After he checked and answered all his emails, he decided to hell with it, and sent Carly a text. If he was just going to end up thinking about her all day, he might as well get to talk to her.

Anthony:

Checking in to see how everything is going?

She responded immediately, which shocked him

Carly:

I just left the school. I got Reed all enrolled and situated. They let him start today and he was excited.

Anthony:

Wow, that's great.

Carly:

I know. He really seemed happy to be going to school. What 6-year-old likes school?

Anthony:

It takes all kinds.

Carly:

Any interest in having lunch with me? I know you're busy but I am coming to Woodbridge to pick up a few things, so I'll be close.

Anthony:

When and where?

Carly:

Baxter's at noon.

Baxter's was a local burger place right around the corner from his office. A day that had started with not knowing when he'd get to see Carly again, was now turning out to be great.

He kept himself busy and at five till twelve, walked down the street to Baxter's. He spotted her almost as soon as he walked in, sitting at a table in the back. His heartbeat sped up and it took all he had not to run full speed toward her.

She spotted him coming toward her and her face lit up in a huge smile. The fact he had that effect on her, that just seeing him made her smile, was all he needed in the world.

Instead of sitting, he went directly to her, bent and kissed her lips. It was quick, just a hello, but he needed the contact after two days without it.

"Well, hello to you too," she said when he pulled away and sat down.

"I had to get that out of the way or I wouldn't have been able to concentrate on anything else."

"Hey, I'm not complaining. Kinda wished it would've lasted longer."

He exhaled and shifted in his seat. "Maybe we don't flirt while in a public place. Unless you want to end up on top of this table. Naked."

She stuck her tongue out at him. "You...are no fun."

He raised an eyebrow, but didn't comment. "Tell me about your weekend?"

"God, where do I start? He's a freaking great kid, Anthony. I don't know how or why but he is. And he's funny for a six-year-old. He has a real sense of humor."

"What kind of things did you guys do?"

"I took him to the studio and he loved it. He thought the mirrors everywhere were awesome. He also got to meet Leah and Mel, who agree, he is an amazing kid. Ryan and I took him to lunch and then we explored the town a little. Went down to the dock at my aunt and uncle's so he could check out the water. He was dying to go out on a boat, but I was able to sway him from that. At least for a little bit."

"What's Ryan like?" He tried to keep the jealousy from his voice, but could tell from her smirk, he hadn't succeeded.

"He's nice. Busy. He's always on his phone, either talking, texting, or emailing. I can see why having Reed would be difficult."

"What does Ryan do?"

"He's a tax attorney in Baltimore, and as far as I can tell, he works a ton and has no life."

He nodded. He hated being jealous. Hated it. But this guy had gotten to spend the whole weekend with her and he'd slept in her house.

"I told him about you."

That made him pay attention. "You did?"

"I wanted to know what he thought about me introducing you to Reed and maybe you spending time with the two of us."

"You want me to meet Reed?"

"I think it's going to be inevitable since I plan on seeing you. A lot."

He smiled. "What did Ryan think?"

"I love how you just ignore when I say poignant things. You have a real skill for that."

"Since I learned it from you, you shouldn't really have a problem with it."

She scoffed. "You were fluent in it before I ever came along."

"That's why we're perfect for each other."

She rolled her eyes. "To answer your question, Ryan was on board. He thinks I shouldn't have to stop my life, and as long as you aren't a 'flash in the pan' – his words, not mine – it's fine." She looked down as if there was something riveting on the table. "We aren't are we? Just a flash in the pan?"

He hated that she had insecurities, especially when it came to him or them. He liked her strong and arrogant. "Look at me." He reached across the table and took her hand. "I'd make you promises today if I thought you were ready for them, but since you aren't, just know this, I want to be with you and no one else. And, if you feel the same, we can take this one day at a time."

"I do, I just have no idea of the direction my life is going right now. But I do know I don't want to stop seeing you. I feel more alive with you than I do any other time."

He caressed her hand. "While I love hearing that, I'd love it more if you could feel alive, all day, every day, whether I'm around or not."

She gave a little nod. "I'm working on it."

They ordered their lunch, talking about all things Reed while they ate. He loved watching her light up with excitement while she spoke. They were just about finished when his sister walked in.

"Hey Addison," Carly called her over.

"I wondered where you ran off too," Addison said to him as she sat down. "One minute you were there and then, poof, you were gone."

He rolled his eyes. "You aren't my boss, so contrary to what you believe, I do not have to run everything I do by you."

She waved him off. "Like I care where you go."

Carly was laughing across the table from him. "What's so funny?"

"You two are. I have no idea how you guys get anything done at your office with all your bickering."

"We don't always bicker," he said.

"Umm, yeah, we do," Addison contradicted.

Leave it to her to make him look like an ass.

"Addison, I am so sorry I had to cancel last week. My life has gone from uncomplicated to complete chaos in a matter of days."

"No worries. I figure it had to be something big."

"If you call finding out I have a six-year-old brother big, then yeah."

Addison's eyes widened in shock. "Yeah...that would be big."

"It's a crazy long story but basically, I am caring for him right now." She paused and Tony watched as she seemed to ponder how much to say. "His mom – my mom – died in a car crash. His dad too. He was left in the care of his uncle, but he needed help, and well, here I am."

Addison looked at him and then back to Carly. "Wow. I don't even know what to say."

Carly shrugged. "He's a great kid and deserves the best."

"If you need any help...seriously, call me. I am great with kids. Ask Tony?"

He nodded his confirmation. "She is. Babysat every kid in the neighborhood growing up."

"I'll keep that in mind."

After several more minutes of talking, Carly indicated she needed to leave. With his hand on her back, he led her out of the restaurant and out to the sidewalk.

"Thanks for making time for me today." She looked up at him, her dark lashes obscuring her sapphire blue eyes.

"Always." He moved closer. Placing his lips on hers, he kissed her sweetly, pulling back when he got the urge to go deeper. They were in public and he didn't want to embarrass her in any way.

"Come by tomorrow night. For dinner. You can meet Reed."

"What if I also come by your place for lunch?" He didn't want to make their relationship all about sex, but he'd die if he didn't get to be with her again and soon.

Licking her lips, she smirked. "A little needy aren't you?"

"When it comes to you, absolutely."

She backed away and then turned, walking away.

"That wasn't an answer," he called out laughing.

Stopping, she looked over her shoulder. "If you don't know by now that I'd never say no to you, then you aren't as smart as I thought you were." She looked forward and continued walking away.

He was hard and horny and tomorrow was a long way away.

Fuck his life.

He was finishing up for the day when a text came through from Logan.

Logan:

Gayle's, 7:00?

Tony:

I'll be there.

Thank God for his friends. If he'd have had to spend another night alone in his house with nothing to do but think about Carly, he was going to go mad. Or madder than he already was. He locked up the office and ran home to change. He made it to Gayle's a few minutes before seven and found Logan already at the bar.

"You starting without me?" Tony slapped him on the back and pulled out the stool next to him, sitting down.

"I came from my mom's and didn't want to go home first." As he spoke, Tony nodded to the bartender for a beer.

"How's your mom doing?" Logan and Brandon's mom was amazing. So amazing in fact that she was going to run Logan's new art gallery.

"Busy. There is a lot of organization that goes into owning and starting a business. Thank God I have her."

"It's a pain, but well worth it in the end." Tony remembered when he'd started his security company. It had been a lot of hard work and a ton of paperwork. But he'd done it with the help of his parents and even his sister. Having family was a blessing, even if it didn't always seem that way.

"There's Bran," Logan said. "Why don't we get a table so we can eat? I'm starving."

"Fine by me."

They met Brandon before he could sit, and they found an empty table.

"You just getting off work?" he asked Brandon.

"Yeah," he signaled to a waitress and when she walked over, ordered a beer. "I love summer, but I am glad fall is here and tourist season is over. My job is easier in the winter."

"Your job is easy anyway," Logan said. "We live in Cedarville. Nothing bad ever happens here."

"Do you not remember just eight months ago when Leah had a stalker?"

Logan leaned back in his chair balancing it on two legs. "That was an isolated event. And thanks to Tony here, most of the businesses and homes around town are secure."

He saluted them with his beer. "I do what I can."

"Have you talked to Carly today," Bran asked, changing the subject.

"We had lunch."

"Leah says Reed is a great kid and Carly is really good with him."

"You guys haven't met him yet?"

"No," Logan said. "She is trying not to overwhelm him so she was thinking of maybe planning a run-in with each of us at separate times. What about you?"

"I haven't met him yet either. Although, I think I am going over for dinner tomorrow." He said it cautiously, hoping neither of them would be mad or upset that he might be meeting Reed first.

"It's probably good for you to meet him, if you are going to be spending a lot of time with Carly," Brandon said.

"I'm a little nervous."

"Really? Why?" Logan asked

"What if he hates me?" This was something he had been thinking of since the first moment Carly had told him about Reed. He had no real interaction with kids and wasn't sure how to treat them.

"You're worried if he doesn't like you then Carly will choose him over you?" Brandon said.

"Well shit," he said. "I hadn't been, but I am now."

"Doesn't matter either way," Logan said. "Reed will like you."

"How the hell are you so confident in that?"

Logan shrugged. "Kids like people who are honest with them and who are fun. You're both of those things."

"I appreciate the vote of confidence but I'm still not sure." He sipped his beer quietly and listened to them continue to talk. To Carly, he'd made sure to put on a happy face and pretend that all was okay, when really on the inside, he was all tied up. He wanted to be with her. Forever, if the choice was his, but how would her having Reed fit into that? Would Reed like him, would Ryan like him? Was Carly even going to have Reed after this first month?

But the biggest question of all was...did she want to be with him forever?

Chapter 11

Carly was a frazzled mess. Nothing in the last twenty-four hours had gone as planned. It had all started when she'd picked Reed up from school and found out he had not had a great day. He'd apparently had a meltdown after he'd accidentally spilled a carton of milk during lunch. Both the teacher and principal were unable to find out why, and when she herself had tried, he'd just closed up. He didn't want to talk and instead spent most the night avoiding her.

She hadn't wanted to yell at him and not knowing what else to do, she just let him be. When morning came and she got him up to go to school, he went reluctantly, barely speaking a word. When she had picked him up again, he was acting the same way.

Now, it was ten minutes until Anthony was due to be there for dinner, and Reed was still not talking to her. She had to do something.

"Reed, can you come down here please?" She waited for him to come downstairs and join her. He stepped off the bottom step and looked at her. "Come sit," she patted the chair at the table next to her.

Fear showed on his face and she wondered, not for the first time, what his life had been like before.

"Are you going to send me away now?" His small, fragile voice cut through her heart.

"What? No. Why would you say that?"

"I always get in trouble if I do something wrong and my mom and dad would just leave me in my room."

She was seething on the inside but she didn't want to frighten Reed. "Is that why you have been hiding from me since yesterday? You think I am mad at you?"

"I spilled the milk all over and the teacher was real mad. When mom got real mad, I'd just stay quiet and hide so she'd forget about me."

Her heart broke. "Reed, I will never be so mad at you that I will want you to leave." She wasn't sure how to tell a six-year-old there were bad people or how to make him understand, so she tried her best.

"Mistakes happen. I am not going to be angry with you for spilling milk or breaking something. I never want you to go hide. I might get mad and yell, but it won't be because I don't want you."

"I like it here and I don't want to leave." His eyes were wide with hope.

"I like having you here and I don't want you to leave. And Ryan feels the same way. We are both new to this taking care of a kid thing. We're going to need your help to get us through."

"You need my help?" His eyes lit up.

"Yup. I have no idea what I'm doing and I'm sure to make lots of mistakes. If I do, are you going to leave me?"

"Never. I like it here. I have toys here."

She was so angry with her mom and Rob that, if they were still alive, she would track them down and kill them. They brought this sweet, innocent child into the world and then just neglected him. His comment about having toys, about did her in.

"Can you do me a favor? Talk to me when you are sad or mad or unhappy. I want to know so I can help."

He nodded. "Can I have a cookie now?"

She ruffled his hair. "Sure."

Kids, it seemed, could put their anger away immediately. If only adults did the same.

There was a knock on the door and she assumed it was Anthony. Reed was still in the kitchen, so she walked to the door.

When she opened it, her whole body relaxed in the same way it did every time she saw him.

"Hi," he said, his deep voice music to her ears.

Opening the door, she let him in. "Before you meet Reed," she whispered, "you should know we just had a little meltdown. But I think he and I have worked it out and now are on the same page."

"Is everything okay?"

"I think it's going to be." They walked further into the house. "Reed, can you come over here and meet my friend?"

Reed, a cookie in tow, walked to her and Anthony.

"This is Anthony." As she said it, she realized it might be better if she went a different way. "Tony. This is Tony and he is my very good friend." She looked up at him from where she was squatting on the floor.

Kneeling down to join them, Anthony held out his hand. "It's extremely nice to meet you, Reed." Reed accepted Anthony's hand and shook it firmly.

"Is it okay if I have dinner with you and Carly?"

Reed nodded shyly. "She makes you wash your hands before you eat."

Anthony laughed and stood. "I'm cool with washing my hands."

Carly held in her laugh. "Why don't you go play, Reed and I will call you when the food is ready." Reed ran off and she watched him go.

"Seems like you are getting the hang of this," Anthony said.

Turning toward him she took him in. Jeans, t-shirt and gym shoes, his standard attire, but he wore it well. So well, she had a hard time keeping her hands to herself. "What makes you say that?"

"My mom used to make me wash my hands before dinner too."

She lifted an eyebrow. "And that makes me qualified to raise a child?"

"It's that you care enough to remind him to wash his hands." He took a step closer to her. "I'm guessing he hasn't had very many people care about him."

She swallowed and wet her lips with her tongue. He was standing merely a foot from her and he smelled delicious. So delicious she had to hold herself back from licking him. "I'm starting to come to the same conclusion."

He reached out a hand and smoothed a stray hair from her face. "Wanna tell me about the meltdown?"

She nodded. "I do, but first..." she didn't finish her sentence, instead she grabbed him by the back of the head and sealed her lips to his. She needed this. Him and her, together. It just felt...right. And when he wasn't around and she couldn't touch or kiss him, it sucked.

Neither one deepened the kiss, both of them content to just be together, kissing. She pulled back and looked up at him. "It's ridiculous how much that makes me feel better."

"I know how you feel." He smiled down at her.

Letting go of him, she took a step back. "I need to check on dinner." He followed her into the kitchen and grabbed himself a beer from the fridge.

"Need any help?"

"Nah, it's all done, just want to put the rolls in to warm them."

As she moved around the kitchen, he took a seat at the counter. "Wanna know something crazy?" he asked when her back was turned.

"How crazy?" she asked without turning to look at him. "Your mom has a secret kid and he is now living with you crazy, or you have a tattoo on your ass crazy?"

She heard him laugh. "Since I've seen your ass and know it is, in fact, tattoo-free, it's definitely not that one."

She turned and found him staring at her. "Thank God for that." Leaning back against the counter she motioned for him to go on.

"I was crazy nervous about meeting Reed." His admission floored her. He'd seemed so calm when she'd asked, although to be fair, he was always calm. Except for the few times he wasn't. And those had all been about his feelings for her.

"Why?"

"What if he hated me? How would that have worked?"

"First," she walked over to stand in front of him, only the counter between them, "I don't think there is a person in this world who hates you. Hell, I tried to be that person and look how it turned out. Second, I've realized something this week. I deserve to be happy. And Anthony," she leaned forward, elbows on the counter, face-to-face with him, "you make me happy. I wouldn't give that up."

His eyes flared and he started to speak, but Carly heard footsteps and turned to see that Reed had come downstairs.

"I'm hungry," he said.

"Dinner is pretty much ready. Why don't you and Tony set the table?"

"I don't know how to do that." He hung his head, but before she could comfort him, Anthony was up and doing his thing.

"That's what I'm here for. Let's go grab all the things we need and I'll show you how it's done."

Thank God for Anthony.

She watched as Anthony instructed Reed on what they'd need and then, eventually, how they set the table. Her heart was ready to burst through her chest. This could be her life. Hers and Anthony's, and any children they had. And Reed. Always Reed. Every night, they could have dinner together and Anthony would be there to help set the table and help the kids with homework.

When had she allowed herself to fall in love with him?

She rolled her eyes at her own thought. Who the hell was she kidding? She'd been in love with him since she'd met him. Even when she'd hated him.

The question now was, what was she going to do about it? She'd just finished telling him she deserved to be happy. So no way was she going to hide the fact that she loved him and wanted more. Wanted everything really.

He'd either stick or he'd run. The choice was his.

After dinner, the three of them played a rousing game of Chutes and Ladders. Anthony made sure Reed felt involved and had fun. Another reason for her to love him. After the game, Carly offered to read a story to him before bedtime.

"Could Tony do it?" his little voice asked.

Carly looked over at Anthony who said, "Heck yeah, I can."

"Brush your teeth, put your pj's on and pick your book. Tony will be up in a few minutes."

Reed ran up the stairs and before Carly could stop herself she blurted, "I love you. It's annoying and it's early and I have no idea what the hell I'm doing with Reed, but I can't help it." She turned to look at him. "I love you and if you don't love me back I'm praying that a huge hole opens up in this floor and swallows me."

She never took her eyes off his even though she wanted to badly. His lips were tilted up in sort of a half-smirk and she couldn't make it out. Was it bad or good?

Quietly, not sure she wanted him to hear her or not she said, "Say something."

"I didn't think you were ready," he said when he finally spoke. "I thought it was the wrong time, that you had too much going on. But, I can see I was wrong. I shouldn't have waited, shouldn't have made you say it first. You deserve more...everything."

She knew what he was saying, could tell he loved her too. But he was taking too long to say the words. "Tell me now. And hurry."

He took one of her hands in his and cupped her cheek with the other. "I love you, Carly. More than I ever thought it was possible to love another person."

She sighed and let herself relax. "Why do we always have to do things the hard way?"

He kissed her softly on the lips. "Easy is overrated." He pulled away. "I better go read a bedtime story. Don't change your mind in the time I'm gone."

His hand slid from hers as he took a step away from her and toward the stairs. She wanted to move, maybe go sit on the couch, but part of her wanted to stay in the exact spot where Anthony had said I love you for the first time.

It was stupid, she knew that. It was even more stupid because she wasn't a sentimental person. But, this moment seemed important to her. She hoped it was because it was going to be the last, first I love you, she would ever have.

That should scare her shitless. It didn't. Surprisingly, it gave her strength.

A strength that told her everything was going to be alright. A strength that told her this was right, that Anthony's love was the real deal.

Finally able to move, she went to the kitchen and finished cleaning up from dinner. When she finished, she grabbed a water and sat on the couch. Normally she'd turn on the TV, but her mind did not want to be numbed. She wanted to remember everything about the night.

When she heard footsteps coming down the stairs, she turned her head to look. "He go down okay?"

"Easy as pie." He slid beside her on the couch and laid his arm across her shoulders pulling her into his side. She felt him kiss the top of her head and she snuggled in closer.

"I'm sorry I was such a bitch to you when we first met."

He laughed, his whole body shaking. "If you'd have fallen at my feet and professed your love for me on day one, I'm not sure we'd be where we are now."

Looking up at him, she asked, "So, it was the thrill of the chase that made you love me?"

Turning fully to look at her, he caressed her hands in his. "No. It's more than that. One of the reasons I love you is your tenacity. The way you question everything, and the fire in your attitude to always make sure you are doing the right thing. If we had gotten together immediately, I would have never known about those qualities I love."

"So, basically, you're a masochist."

"If it means I get you, then, yeah, I am."

She slapped his arm. "Hey."

Moving his face in closer to hers, she felt his breath on her mouth. "I love you." His eyes held steady to hers until he lowered his mouth the last inch and kissed her. Gripping the front of his shirt in her fists, she kissed him back with everything she had. She wanted him to feel her love for him through the kiss. She wanted him to know how much he meant to her.

"We have to stop," he mumbled against her lips.

Leaning her forehead against his, she took a deep breath. "While my head knows that, there are other parts of my body that disagree."

"Are you going back to work tomorrow?"

"No, I took the whole week so I could help Reed adjust."

"Since we had to cancel our rendezvous this afternoon, why don't I come by after you drop Reed at school tomorrow?"

"Aren't you sneaky using the word 'rendezvous'?"

"If sneaky is what it takes to be with you right now, then I'm in."

"Since I'll already be out, why don't I come to you? I have this weird need to be in your bed." Saying that made her nervous that he would find her odd, but she was done with holding back.

He closed his eyes. "Thinking of you in my bed with me, is going to keep me up all night."

She laughed. "Twelve hours is going to feel like an eternity."

"I better go." He stood. "Get some sleep and I'll see you tomorrow."

Not getting up, she leaned back against the couch. "Thank you for coming over tonight and for being so nice to Reed."

"He's a sweet kid. It's easy to be nice to him." He walked to the door. "Tomorrow," he said as he turned the knob and opened the door. "Tomorrow, I'll show you how much I love you."

He left before she could speak, leaving her staring after him. She was tempted to follow him out and say screw the fact that she had a six-year-old boy living with her. But she knew it was a bad idea. Plus, twelve hours wasn't that long.

Or so she hoped.

Chapter 12

Tony woke from what he imagined was only about an hour of sleep. When he'd gotten home the previous night, he'd been too wired to sleep. The woman he loved, loved him back.

It was a miracle if he'd ever seen one.

She'd just about shocked the hell out of him when she blurted it out. But, since that was one of the things he loved about her, he came back to reality fast. He would have loved to stay with her and make love to her there in her house, but that just wasn't an option. Not yet, with Reed living with her.

After spending time with Reed, he was right there with Carly in wanting to protect and take care of him. While he'd been reading him a bedtime story, Reed had mentioned that until he'd met Ryan, no one had ever read a book to him. That had made him angry that anyone would treat a small child like that.

Reed was bright and funny. How his parents had just ignored him, was beyond Tony.

Drinking his second cup of coffee, he texted his sister to let her know he wouldn't be in the office for a few hours. He had no installs or off-site meetings, so spending a few hours with Carly wasn't going to put him too far behind.

Taking his coffee into his bedroom, he picked up some stray clothes and ripped the sheets from his bed. He wasn't a dirty person but he also wasn't someone who changed the sheets on a weekly basis. But for Carly, he'd change them every damn day.

After making the bed with clean linens, he threw the dirty ones in the wash just as he heard a knock on the door. He tried to take his time walking to the front of his house, but it was useless when he knew who was on the other side.

When he opened the door, Carly stood, looking gorgeous as ever in only jeans and a Dragonfly Dance sweatshirt.

"Hey," he said, reaching out his hand and pulling her inside. He didn't want to waste a minute of their time together.

"In a hurry, are you?"

"You have no idea." He kept her hand in his and loosely pulled her to his room, her laughing all the way.

"Are you even going to give me time to get naked or are we making love fully dressed?"

Finally in his room, he turned to face her. "Oh you're getting naked but, if you like those clothes, you better remove them fast."

She lifted an eyebrow and glared at him. "A little caveman, don't ya think?"

"Baby, you haven't seen anything yet." He stripped his shirt off over his head and dropped it on the floor. "You're not moving."

A wicked smile lit up her face. "I'm trying to decide if it would be hot or annoying if you followed through and ripped them off."

He cocked his head to the side. "In about ten seconds you're going to have your answer."

She rolled her eyes and started removing her clothes. He did the same, unbuttoning and lowering his jeans but leaving his boxers on. Both of them now only in their underwear, he stalked toward her, forcing her back onto his bed. Climbing over top of her, he kissed his way up her stomach.

"You are so fucking sexy," he growled as his tongue flicked out and licked her belly button.

She was wiggling under him and he knew that going slow was torture. It was torture for him too. But he wanted to savor her and show her just how much he loved her.

When he reached her bra-clad breasts, he bypassed them and moved to her neck. Slowly licking a path up to her mouth until he settled in for a kiss that would hopefully, drive her insane. When her hands gripped his ass and her nails dug into his skin through his boxers, he knew he was on the right course.

When she tried to speed things along, he did his best to hold strong and go slow. Kissing from her mouth to her ear, he nipped her lobe softly, loving when she moaned.

"I might die before you get to the good stuff."

He chuckled. "It's all good stuff, baby." Moving back down her body, he reached under her back, forcing her to arch off the bed, so he could unclasp her bra. Using his other hand, he pushed the material down off her breasts, baring them to his eyes. He knew she hated that they were small, but to him they were perfect. He feathered his fingers on the underside of one breast until he finally came in contact with her nipple. Rolling it between his thumb and index finger, he marveled at the flush of red that covered her skin.

Grabbing his wrist in her hand, she growled, "Put your fucking mouth on me."

With a smile covering his face, he lowered his head. "As you wish." His tongue touched her hardened nipple and she moaned. Slowly at first, he teased it, kissing and licking lightly. When her moans grew louder and her body started squirming under his, he added suction and teeth. He continued his torture on the other side before moving further down her body.

When he reached her panty covered pussy, he slid them down her legs in one swift motion, with her helping to kick them off. He knew she was wet and when his fingers dipped between her folds he was rewarded with a shout. Not wanting to wait to taste her, and not sure he even could, he spread her with his fingers and licked her. After just one taste he lost control and began to devour her with everything he had. He used his whole arsenal: tongue, teeth, lips, and fingers to bring her pleasure. And, when she pressed her pussy harder into his mouth and came, he felt proud he was the one who had taken her there.

Slipping out from between her legs, he shucked his boxers and reached for the condom he'd set on his nightstand. He rolled it on before settling back over top of her.

"What if I wanted to be on top?" she joked lazily. in a satisfied voice.

"Then by all means." He rolled them both so she was now on top.

A wicked gleam crossed her face. "You know how much I like to be in control." She slipped her hand between them, finding his cock hard and ready to go. Sliding her body down, she rubbed the tip of his cock against her drenched pussy. He didn't want to take charge, but fuck if he wasn't having a hard time not doing just that.

"Is this what you want?" She grinned, still rubbing his cock against her.

"I want more." His hands found their way to her hips for some leverage.

Slipping the tip of him inside her, he watched as she closed her eyes and moaned. The look on her face was one he never wanted to forget. It was pure ecstasy.

Finally, she engulfed him completely and began to move. She started on her knees lifting herself up and down with his hips and hands helping out. Then she maneuvered so she was flat on her feet.

He almost came just looking at her in that position. He knew she was limber from years of dancing but, he'd never even thought how that would transfer over to sex.

Stupid him.

As she continued to move up and down, he became unable to think or focus on anything but her and his impending release. His balls felt like they were going to explode, and while he wanted that, he also wanted badly for this to go on forever. Or at least until she came.

Then she blew his mind even more by leaning back, her arms supporting her and straightening her legs out along his torso. His control was no match for her flexibility. He came instantly, grunting and gripping her hips.

He felt her spasm on top of him and watched as she too rode out her orgasm.

As their breathing slowed, Carly sat back up and then slipped off of him, curling into his side. He didn't want to move, but unfortunately, he had to take care of the condom. She groaned a sound of annoyance when he sat up.

"Don't go."

"I'll be right back." In his bathroom, he disposed of the condom quickly so he could rejoin her in his bed.

He found her still on her side, so he scooted right in and wrapped his arms around her. He'd love nothing more than to stay in bed with her all day, but they both had priorities that couldn't be put off.

"Your bed is comfy," she murmured against his ear.

"You're just tired. Anything would be comfortable."

"True story."

He laughed. "What do you have going on today?" He stroked her hair.

"Not much this morning. When Reed gets off school, I am taking him to meet my dad." She shifted. "I think it's time."

"Is your dad still doing okay with this whole situation?"

She looked up at him. "My dad is the most even-keeled person I know. He's always taken everything in stride and this is no different." She bit her lip. "He's pretty amazing."

"His daughter is pretty amazing herself." He lowered his face and kissed her lips.

When he would have pulled back, she lingered, but kept it light. "I'd invite you to dinner again, but I think we are going to eat at McDonald's with dad."

"Carly, I understand that Reed is where your focus needs to be. You aren't going to hurt my feelings by not inviting me over every night." The words he spoke were true, even if he absolutely wanted to be with her every night.

She sat up, leaned back against the pillow. and sighed. "I know you get it. It's one of the reasons it was so hard not to fall in love with you.

I think I am the one having a problem with it. I want you, and I want Reed, and I want my dance studio. Not to mention, I want to spend time with my family and Leah and Mel. How the hell do people do this?"

He scooted up the bed and pulled the sheet with him so they could cover themselves. Not that he minded her sitting on his bed naked. He'd prefer it actually. But he wanted to make her comfortable while they talked.

"They do it with help. Once Reed gets more acclimated, you'll be able to leave him with someone for a few hours. Aren't you going to have to do that anyway when you go back to work next week?"

"I was planning on taking him and letting him hang in the office, but now that you mention it, I'm guessing he might hate that."

"Probably not at first because it will be a new experience. But every day would be pretty boring for a six-year-old." He paused, letting his next words come slowly." "I'd be happy to take him once a week if you wanted?"

He expected her to look shocked or unsure. Instead, she smiled a huge grin. "Seriously? That would be awesome. Reed really liked you. You were all he talked about this morning. Tony this and Tony that." She was sideways on the bed and her hands were moving a mile a minute as she spoke.

"He talked about me?" Tony wasn't sure what to think of that. He'd never spent much time with kids, and until last night, wasn't even sure how to talk to them. But Reed had made it easy. Tony had just gone with his gut instinct and thought back to himself as a six-year-old and how he would have wanted adults to talk to him.

"It seems like you made an impression. You're like a superhero to him."

He wasn't sure what to say. He'd never had a kid look up to him. "He's a great kid and I had fun hanging out and reading to him."

"If you really mean it, I will totally take you up on watching him one of the nights I'm at work."

"Pick the night and let me know." He glanced at the clock. "I should probably get up and head to work. Addie has a meeting soon and I promised I'd be in before she left."

"Any chance you'd care if I took a short nap here?" She gave him a crooked smile.

Kissing her forehead and then her lips he said, "Stay as long as you want."

After a shower and a mind-numbing kiss from Carly before she slept, he left the house and headed for his office. He was happier than he could ever remember being, and he had her to thank for that. The woman was a marvel. A marvel who loved him.

Life was fucking fantastic.

He barely made it to his office before Addie left. "You heading out?" he asked when he saw her.

"In a few. How was your morning?" She said it with a voice that told him she knew exactly how his morning had been.

"Pretty standard," he said with a straight face.

"You're an ass." She flipped him off as he passed by on the way to his office.

"Takes one to know one." Since they'd been kids, they'd always picked on each other and had silly banter. Things hadn't changed much as adults.

He spent several solitary hours writing up a new bid, designing an install, and sending out invoices. It was after two when he came up for air. Needing sustenance, he walked across the street to the burger joint and ordered some food. He took it to go and went back to his office to eat. When he was almost finished, he heard the ding of the front door and then Logan's voice.

"Tony, you here?"

"In my office," he shouted around the last bite of his burger. Logan strolled in looking relaxed as usual.

"I wasn't sure if I'd find you actually in today or if you'd be out in the field."

"It's a rare day with no appointments."

Logan sat down across from him and lazily crossed one leg over top of the other. "I'm ready to talk security for the gallery."

Tony had been waiting for his friend to come to him with this request. The gallery was decent sized but more than that, it was going to house millions of dollars in art. Being in charge of security was a big deal.

"I already have some ideas." He opened his desk drawer and pulled out a folder which held specs and ideas he'd been working on in his spare time.

"Damn dude," Logan said as he took the folder from him, "you are always one step ahead, aren't you?"

Tony shrugged. "I knew you'd need security with all that art."

"People are already starting to send me pieces and I'm keeping them at my house for now since it's more secure." He flipped through the pages. "This looks great."

"I need to come out and really assess the place, so those aren't exact numbers."

Logan pulled his keys from his pocket and removed a key from the ring. "Take this key and come whenever it's convenient for you. If possible, I'd love to get going on this right away."

"I'll make it a top priority."

"How's Carly treating you?"

Tony smiled at just the mention of her name. "Amazing." It wasn't a strong enough word for how much he loved being with her, but it was the first one that came out.

"I know she can be a hard-ass but she's a good person deep down."

"You don't have to sell me on Carly's good traits. She and I are good...and in love." He sure hoped she wasn't planning on hiding their love because if so, he'd just gone and spilled the beans.

"Seriously? She told you she loves you?"

He nodded. "You sound surprised?"

"Don't get me wrong, man, I was always on your side and I like you two together, but honestly I never thought she'd get her head out of her ass long enough to see it."

"You and me both. But, if I've learned anything about Carly in the last few months, it's that she has to come to things in her own time. If I would have pushed months ago, we might not be where we are today."

"You sir, are a wise and brave man."

Tony laughed. "Don't forget patient."

"That too." Logan stood. "Oh, how'd it go meeting Reed?"

Tony stood too and walked him out. "The kid's pretty cute and really sweet considering all he has been through."

"That's pretty much what Melanie said. Bran and I are going over later tonight to meet him per Carly's request. Any tips?"

"Just treat him normally. He may be six, but he has an old soul."

They shook hands, Logan clapping him on the back. "Take it easy, man, and we'll talk soon."

Back in his office, Tony started laying out more plans for Logan's gallery. This was going to be a huge undertaking and he couldn't wait to get his hands dirty.

Chapter 13

Dinner with her dad and Reed had gone better than anticipated. Her dad had been amazing and Reed took to him right away. Afterward, she and Reed met Logan and Brandon at her house so they could both finally meet him too. And, same as her dad and Anthony, Reed loved them right away. She didn't know the situation with how he grew up, and whether or not Rob had ever been around. But, it seemed like Reed loved attention from men, and that led her to believe he hadn't been.

She'd just put Reed to bed when she heard the front door open. All of her friends had keys and knew the alarm code, so it could've been any one of them. Walking downstairs, she found Leah and Mel, bottles of wine in tow.

"Walk in like you own the place, why don't ya?" She went straight to the kitchen and pulled three wine glasses down.

"I do happen to own the place," Mel said

The house had belonged to Mel's grandparents and when they passed away, it fell to her. She and Carly had lived in it for the last six years together. That is, until Melanie moved in with Logan last month. Now Melanie was renting the place to Carly for as long as she wanted. And renting was a strong word. The reality was Mel wouldn't take any money from her, even money that would cover the cost of property taxes. Carly felt bad at first, but Melanie and Logan had reassured her this was what they wanted. They never planned to sell the house, since it was part of Melanie's life and she loved it, but eventually they would rent it out. But, only if Carly ever wanted to move.

"Oh what do I owe the pleasure of your company?" Carly set the glasses on the counter as Leah was opening a bottle of wine.

"We wanted a little girl time and to check in and see how you were doing?" Leah popped the cork and filled all three glasses.

"I don't know about her," Mel pointed to Leah, "but I came because I want to know all about you and Tony and the hot sex."

"You are like a child," Leah said, taking her first sip.

Carly laughed. "Come on, we might as well go sit down."

"Brandon said he and Logan's meeting with Reed went well," Leah said after they all sat down.

"That kid kinda amazes me," Carly said, meaning it completely. "Other than a small meltdown the other day, he takes everything in stride and doesn't seem to hate life as much as he should. Hell, my situation with my mom and Rob practically shaped my whole existence, but not Reed."

"What was his meltdown about? Leah asked.

Carly took a sip of wine and pulled her legs up under her body. "He spilled milk at school and freaked out. Apparently, if he did something like that before, he'd have gotten in trouble and was sent to his room where he was left for who knows how long." She paused long enough to control her emotions because it still pissed her off. "He asked me if I was going to send him away." Her voice cracked and before she knew what was happening, tears were pooling in her eyes.

"I fucking hate that woman," Mel sneered. "I hated her when we were twelve and she made you miss my birthday party for no reason. And, then again when we were sixteen and she accused you of smoking pot because your dad found it in the house, but we both knew it was hers. I thought the thing with Rob sealed my hate for her, but I was wrong. What she's done to that sweet boy is beyond reprehensible. She was a monster and didn't deserve you or Reed."

Silence settled around them. Carly had no argument for Melanie's hate. She agreed with everything she said and felt exactly the same way. For days she'd been wondering if maybe, in death, her hatred for her mom might go away. Did refusing to forgive a dead woman make her a bad person?

"I only met your mom that one time," Leah said interrupting her thoughts, "but I'm with Mel." Leah reached over and hugged her. "Reed is lucky to have you, Carls."

She shrugged. "I kinda think I might be the lucky one."

"How's Tony doing with all this?"

She smiled. "He's a natural with Reed. After one night, Reed worships him and has barely stopped talking about him."

"What about you?" Leah asked. "Do you worship Tony?" Carly knew she was joking but that didn't stop her from answering honestly.

"I love him, so yeah."

"Wait, wait, wait." Mel held her hand up in a stop motion. "I know we've joked about you loving him before, but you've never said it like that. Are you, for real, in love with him?"

"As real as can be since I told him." Both girls shrieked and Carly had to cover her ears.

"I don't think I ever believed this day would actually come," Leah said, a shocked look on her face. "Tell us the whole story?"

"It just happened last night while he was here for dinner. After we ate, we played games with Reed before bed. When it came time for his bedtime story, Reed asked if Anthony could do it. At that moment, I just knew. And, in classic Carly fashion, I blurted it out." She rolled her eyes at her own idiocy.

"Did he say it back?" Mel wanted to know.

She nodded. "He did and then he actually apologized for waiting too long and forcing me to say it first." She shook her head in amazement, remembering the moment. "How could I not be in love with a man like that?"

Leah gave a little clap. "Tony's so sweet. If you remember, I've been saying so for months."

"Yeah, yeah, I know I'm the idiot who took her sweet time, but I think it's better this way. We know each other more."

"I have a serious question," Mel said. "Do you make Reed call him Anthony?"

It took a second but both she and Leah burst out laughing. "No you dummy. He calls him Tony."

"Phew." She pretended to wipe her brow. "That would just be weird."

"It's not weird, it's his name."

"Do you call him that during sex?"

Carly raised her eyebrows. "Can I plead the fifth?"

"That's pretty telling," Leah said to Melanie.

"If you two are finished annoying me, can we maybe talk about the studio and what the hell I'm gonna do with Reed while I'm working?"

They put their heads together and came up with a plan. Anthony was going to do Mondays and also pick him up on her short night on Tuesday where she only taught until six. Leah was going to watch him at the studio on Wednesdays and then her dad was going to do Thursdays. That only left Friday for her to figure out. She'd see how the week went and make a decision as they got closer. She still had several options including her aunt and Logan and Brandon.

Leah and Melanie left around ten, leaving her alone except for a sleeping six-year-old. The house was quiet as she wandered around locking up and turning off lights. In her bed, she thought back on her day and fell asleep smiling at all the love she had felt from everyone in her life.

Anthony was the last image that came to mind before she finally fell asleep.

By Friday, Carly felt like she was finally getting into a groove. She knew that would all change when she had to go back to work on Monday, but at least she felt more comfortable all around. Ryan was coming back in for the weekend as promised, even though he mentioned this might be the last weekend he visited until the month was up. Carly didn't want to think that far ahead after the great week she'd had with Reed.

While Ryan was in town, her Aunt Alice was throwing a barbecue at her house in honor of Reed. When she'd first told Reed about it he'd been apprehensive and not sure what to expect. But since then her aunt kept sending pics of all the cool "kid" things she planned on having at the house and now Reed was so excited he couldn't stop talking about it.

Some of the cool things included a bounce house, scooters, a basketball hoop, and tons of balls. Carly had tried to explain to her aunt that Reed wasn't there permanently but she was having none of that. She said all the things she bought could all be used once one of them decided to start having kids of their own.

When she'd told Leah and Melanie that, she'd thought she'd see matching looks of shock on their faces. But instead they both looked wistful and avoided eye contact with her. Kids, it seemed, weren't as far off in their lives as she had originally assumed.

She had some free time while Reed was still in school and before Ryan arrived, so she was outside pulling weeds from around her flowers. It was almost the end of growing season since it was nearing the end of September and Carly hated to pull weeds once it got cold. She was bent over at the waist when she heard a whistle from behind her. Straightening, she turned and found Anthony standing a few feet behind her, arms crossed across his chest.

"That's one fine ass, you got there."

"Get a nice look, did ya?"

Grabbing her hand, he pulled her to him. She lifted her gloved hands and tried not to touch him. "I'm all dirty."

He lowered his head and kissed her. "Does it look like I care?" He continued to kiss her. Pulling the gloves from her hands she finally latched onto him. They'd just seen each other the previous night when he'd come over to have dinner with her and Reed. After Reed had gone to bed they'd made out like teenagers on a first date on her couch. The more time she spent with him the more time she wanted to spend with him.

It was getting harder and harder to be apart.

"I missed you," he murmured into her skin under her ear.

"You just saw me last night."

"It's not enough," he sighed and leaned his head against hers.

"I know." She ran her fingers through his hair. "I hate that we can't spend the night together."

"We'll get there. And if I complain too much, just slap me."

"What if you never complain, can I save the slap for another time?" She winked and stepped back.

"One time offer. Sorry." He laughed as they walked up to the porch. "What time is Ryan getting in?"

Even though he knew Carly had no interest in Ryan and wasn't attracted to him, he always said his name with a slight sneer.

"Around five, I think." Making a quick decision she asked, "Would you want to join us for dinner?"

They sat down on her porch swing. "I'm supposed to have dinner with Addie tonight."

"Bring her. It might do Ryan good to be around people and socialize instead of always working. I've never met a person so in need of a social life as Ryan."

"Are you sure? I don't want to intrude."

"It'll be perfect and as a bonus, I get to spend more time with you."

"Sold." He kissed her lips once more.

"Did you come by for something in particular or just for a few kisses?"

"A few kisses is a reason all on its own, but yes, there was another reason."

"I'm all ears."

"Logan called me this morning to give me a heads up that his mom invited my mom and dad to the barbecue."

"Oh." She wasn't sure what to make of that. "Do you not want them to come?"

"No." He laughed. "I just wasn't sure how you'd feel about it since it will be your first time meeting them and we are together."

"Technically, I met your dad once before but let's set that aside. Are you worried I don't want people to know we are together?"

"We hadn't talked about it and I didn't know what your feelings on it were." He was talking faster than he normally did and wasn't looking her in the eyes.

She smiled. "Anthony Scott, are you unsure of yourself?" She'd never seen him so flustered. It was humbling and made her feel just a little bit better about all the times she was unsure of things.

She didn't give him a chance to answer. "Look at me. When I told you I loved you, that was it. That was the moment, that even if I wanted to keep this between us, which I never did, that was the moment it all went out the window. My dad knows about you and, in case you weren't sure, so does my aunt. And I want them too. Meeting your parents will be an honor and I'd love for them to be there."

He nodded. "So we're clear, I want the whole world to know we are together."

"Then we are in agreement." She stood. "Do you have time to come in or do you have to get back to work right away?"

He looked down at his watch and groaned. "If I don't leave in the next five minutes, I won't be able to make it on time for dinner."

Taking his hand, she led him into her house. "We can do a lot with five minutes."

Chapter 14

Anthony was cutting it close, but he made it to Carly's with two minutes to spare. He'd wanted to go home and change after spending the day at Logan's gallery where there was dust everywhere, but that meant he'd have very little extra time. He'd offered to drive Addie to dinner but she'd insisted on driving herself. Her car was already in the drive when he pulled into Carly's, along with another car he assumed was Ryan's. When he got to the door he lifted his hand to knock but before he could the door flew open.

"Tony!" Reed shouted, arms in the air.

"Hey buddy," Tony said and bent to high five his small hand.

"My Uncle Ryan came to visit me and your sister is here. She told me I could call her Addie but I was the only one allowed to." Tony followed the stream of conversation. He knew Reed was a little kid, but the way he communicated was so similar to Carly's, that he was used to it.

He saw Addison in the kitchen with Carly and nodded hello to them both. Ryan had stood when he walked in.

"You must be Tony," he said and held out his hand for Tony to shake. "Reed has been telling me all about you."

Shaking Ryan's hand, Tony relaxed. The man seemed sincere and didn't seem put off that Reed had taken to him. "It's nice to finally meet you. How was your drive down?"

"Long and boring, but it's worth it to see Reed, especially since I don't think I'll be able to make it again until I pick him up."

"Carly mentioned that. I'm sure Reed is going to miss your visits."

"I'd much rather be here with him than dealing with the client who has me working around the clock."

Addie chose that moment to join them. "Anyone need a drink?" She held two beers in her hands.

Snatching one, he said, "When did you get here?"

"About a half an hour ago. I closed the office and came straight here."

"What is it you do?" Ryan asked.

"I work at Tony's security company. I do pretty much anything from installs to paying the bills."

Ryan was eyeing his sister oddly. "You do security system installs?" The question came out rude as if he couldn't believe she was capable of such a thing.

"I do and I'll have you know I am great at it, right Tony?"

"She sure is." He saluted her with his beer.

"I think you misunderstood me. I wasn't suggesting you weren't capable of doing such a job. I was more commenting on the fact that you don't look old enough to be out of college."

Addie's cheeks reddened, a rare occurrence. "I'm actually twenty-six."

Ryan's eyes went wide in shock. "Wow, okay then. I would never have guessed that."

Tony held back a laugh and excused himself to go and see his girl. Yes, he had just seen her hours ago, but she was the best part of his day.

"Hey sexy," she purred as he got closer. "You smell delicious." She sniffed his neck making him go rock hard.

"A shower will do that." Grabbing her around the waist, he planted a scorching kiss on her, as he ground his hardened length into her, letting her know just how much he missed her.

"Wow," she exhaled when he released her. "What did I do to deserve that?"

"You exist."

"You're a funny guy, Anthony." She turned back to the counter and stirred the hamburger.

"Umm, so I think, maybe, Ryan and Addie are flirting."

"What?" She dropped the spatula in the pan and turned. "How do you know?"

"She blushed, and she never does that, and he seemed confused to learn she was twenty-six. Plus, there's a weird vibe." He waved his hand in the air toward the living room.

"Dammit." She began stirring the meat again. "I want her to find someone, but not someone who doesn't live here. Ryan would be great though. I think deep down he also needs someone in his life."

Coming up behind her, he placed his hands on her shoulders. "Slow your roll. Why don't we let Addie and Ryan worry about their own love lives. We have our hands full with our own."

She turned her head up to his, her face scrunched in, what he'd come to know, as her pouty face. "You are no fun. But I still love you."

"I'd hope so." He bent and gave her lips a small peck. "Do you need any help?"

"Nope, I am almost finished. Take your beer and go entertain those two and Reed."

Back in the living room, he found Reed on the floor playing with Legos and Addie and Ryan on the couch talking and laughing, of all things.

"Can I play," he said to Reed as he sat down next to him.

"Yup." He continued with what he was building and didn't look at Tony.

Together they built blocks for a few minutes until Carly yelled that dinner was ready. They ate with comfortable conversation, everyone joining in, even Reed. After dinner, Reed asked if he could watch his favorite movie, Transformers, in Carly's bed.

Carly looked at them all and shrugged. "Sometimes he likes to hang in my room and watch movies and I let him. Don't judge me."

"I'm not judging you," Ryan said. "I'm in awe of the amazing job you have done in such a short amount of time."

Tony felt the same way. Only now that Ryan had said it, he felt stupid saying virtually the same thing. Instead he climbed the stairs a few minutes after her to have a moment alone. Reed was lounging in her bed with the movie already starting. Carly exited the room when she saw him, but left the door open.

"Did you come to watch the movie too?" She leaned her back against the wall on the outside of her room.

He shook his head from side to side. "I wanted a moment alone with you to tell you how much I love you and admire you."

Her face lit up with a smile. "You didn't have to get me alone to tell me that. In fact, I'd prefer it if you declared your love for me in front of other people."

He raised an eyebrow. "That could be arranged."

Lifting a hand to his face, she stroked the stubble on his chin. "Earlier today wasn't enough time. I need more."

She was talking about that afternoon and their five minutes of groping before he had to bolt and get to work. It hadn't been enough for him either, but they had to take time where they could get it.

"They'll be more, we just have to be patient."

"Have you ever known me to be patient?" She shook her head and laughed. "Come on, let's go back down before Ryan and Addie think we are having sex up here."

"Or...since they are already thinking it, we could just go ahead and do it?"

She slapped his arm. "Get moving." When he walked in front of her she patted his ass.

"Hey, there you guys are," Addison said. "Ryan and I came up with an idea we think you might like."

"Yeah, what's that?" he asked.

Ryan stood. "I was thinking that you guys probably haven't been getting to spend a lot of time together with Reed being here. But what if tonight, you could?"

"What do you mean?" Carly asked.

"What if I stayed here with Reed tonight so you could stay with Tony?"

Tony looked back and forth between Carly and Ryan, not sure if he should take time to hug the guy, or just grab Carly and run.

"What do you think?" Addison said. "It's brilliant, right?"

Carly still hadn't said a word so he spoke. "It has to be Carly's decision." Turning toward her, he lowered his voice so only she could hear him. "We don't have to if you don't want to. I am fine waiting."

She licked her lips slowly. It was torture.

Turning to Ryan she asked, "Are you sure about this? I don't expect it and I don't want to shirk my responsibilities."

"Carly, you did me a huge favor by helping out, and I can see how it was the right thing to do because Reed obviously loves it here, and loves you. But you deserve to have some time for you. Please let me do this."

"You guys...do this," Addison said.

Carly looked at him again and smiled. "You game?"

"Damn straight."

"That settles it," Addison said. "Go get your stuff, Carly and you and Ryan can tell Reed. Tony and I will wait for you down here."

Carly and Ryan ascended up the stairs leaving Tony with his sister.

"Was this your idea?"

"You can't tell me it's not a good one?" Hands on hips, she stared him down.

"I was going to thank you and say you are my new favorite person. But now I'm rethinking that since it'll go to your head." He shook his head and sat down in one of the chairs next to the couch.

She flipped him off and sat on the couch. "So you know, Ryan was in total agreement. It's not like I bullied him into it or anything."

He laughed. "Somehow I doubt that's one hundred percent true. You don't seem to realize your own power."

"If I had any power at all, I wouldn't be friendless and sexless."

"Please," he held up a hand, "I do not want to hear the word sex from you. And you are no longer friendless."

"Only because my big brother fixed that problem."

"All I did was introduce you to some people. You made them like you."

She shrugged. "As if your girlfriend is going to risk her relationship with you by not being friends with me."

He scoffed. "You don't know Carly then. She would not be friends with someone just to please me or anyone. Not her style." He heard steps coming down the stairs and stood. "She's a lot like you in that way."

Carly stepped into the living room with Ryan right behind her. "Reed is all set and thinks it cool he'll have Ryan all to himself for the night."

Tony took a step toward her and reached for the bag she was carrying. "Do you need anything else?"

"Nope." She smiled up at him, a glint in her eyes. "I'm all ready."

"You guys have fun and Reed and I will see you tomorrow."

"Why don't we meet for breakfast?" Tony suggested.

"Good idea," Carly said. "How about IHOP at ten?"

Ryan noded. "See you then."

Carly and Tony walked to the door but when Addison didn't make a move to leave, Tony stopped. "Aren't you leaving, Add?"

"I thought maybe if it was okay with Ryan I would stay and help with Reed until bedtime?" She looked at Ryan who was wide-eyed.

"I – I'd be okay with that." He stuttered out.

"Perfect," Carly announced and pushed him closer to the door. "Have fun and we'll see you tomorrow!"

Tony wasn't sure how he felt about whatever was happening between his sister and Ryan. Sure, he'd joked earlier to Carly about them flirting, but he never actually thought it would become a thing.

"Don't worry about Addison and Ryan," Carly said when they were in his truck. "I kinda cornered him upstairs and told him that if he messed with her, he'd have to answer to me." She raised her eyebrows.

"He assured me he had no plans to mess with her. While he's not dating anyone and finds Addison extremely attractive – his words – he has no time to start anything, and he's not into one night stands."

"I have news for you...all guys are into one night stands."

She cocked her head to the side. "You weren't."

She had him there. "Okay, sure, there are some guys who are already in love with someone and so they refuse to go out and have a one night stand. But Ryan is not in love with anyone as far as we know, and he's definitely not in love with Addison after only meeting her tonight. A one night stand is never off the table."

Carly was quiet on her side of the truck. When he looked over, her lips were pursed as if trying not to laugh.

"What?"

"It's just cute watching you be protective of your grown sister."

"Isn't that my job?"

"Yes, if she needs it and when she's twelve. But in case you haven't noticed, Addison is not twelve, and I'm pretty sure she can take care of herself." She reached out her hand and placed it on his thigh. "Take it from someone who knows...she'll appreciate you more if you let her be her own person."

Carly was an only child but had basically grown up with Logan and Brandon as brothers. And he knew how protective they could be. He'd been surprised as fuck to find out neither of them had had a problem with him pursuing her.

"I'll concede your point...for now." He knew she was probably right, but this was his sister, and it was hard to break old habits.

He gripped her hand which was on his thigh in his, driving the rest of the way to his house just like that. When he pulled into his drive, he'd no sooner turned off the engine when she was across the seat and straddling his lap.

"You know there is a perfectly good bed less than fifty feet from here," he said between kisses.

"We have all night for a bed." She bit his bottom lip and then soothed it with another kiss.

His dick had been semi-hard since the moment she'd said yes to coming home with him, and now with her sitting on top of him, he was fully hard and unsure how he was going to go slow.

That always seemed to be a problem with them. He wanted her too much to take it slow.

Their kisses became urgent and sloppy with Carly grinding down on top of him. Slipping his hands under her shirt, he caressed her skin lightly. Lifting the shirt higher, he stripped it over her head and then pulled the cups of her bra down to give him access to her breasts. She hugged his head tightly as he devoured each breast in his mouth. Her nipples hardened as he teased and tormented her.

"Hurry, hurry," she panted, forcing her hands between them to try and unsnap his jeans. He lifted his head from her chest and together they somehow, in the tiny space, both pulled their pants down far enough.

She was rubbing her wet pussy back and forth on his cock when he remembered he didn't have a condom.

"Fuck," he swore.

"I thought that's what we were getting ready to do?"

"I don't have a condom." He dropped his head back against the seat. "Dammit!"

"Have I forgotten to mention I'm on the pill?"

He snapped his head back up, searching her face for confirmation of what she was saying. "Are you saying what I think you are saying?"

"If you think I am saying we don't need condoms, then yeah." As she spoke she reached between them and slipped the head of his cock inside herself.

"Are you sure?" he gritted out. He was having a hard time breathing and thinking at the same time.

"What do you think," she said as she slid further down on him.

"Holy hell." She felt so perfect wrapped around him, gripping him tightly. "I'm never going to last."

She laughed and began to move. "Okay by me."

As she moved up and down, he gripped her hips and helped. Her hands cupped his head from the back, her fingers digging into his scalp. His mouth connected with hers as she bounced up and down on top of him.

"Oh God," she moaned into his mouth as she came, her walls tightening like a vise around his cock.

He pounded into her faster and harder, coming with a shout and holding her down on top of him.

They were both breathing heavily as they continued their kisses, only slower.

"Now wasn't that better than a bed?"

"Don't know about better, but definitely more inventive."

She laughed and he hardened again, still inside her. "Oh," she cooed and ground down on top of him. "I'm thinking you liked it more than you let on."

He thrust up into her. "What I like is you."

It was another fifteen minutes before they made it inside to his bed and another three hours before they fell to sleep, exhausted.

Chapter 15

Carly woke up, sore in places she'd never been sore, but happier than she could remember. She and Tony had spent several hours involved in sexual acrobatics before falling asleep in each other's arms. The whole night had been amazing and she wished all her nights could be the same. Only she knew they couldn't, at least not while Reed was with her.

"It's too early for you to be thinking so hard. Apparently I didn't do a good enough job wearing you out last night."

She turned and found Anthony awake and staring at her from his side. He had two days worth of stubble on his face making him even sexier than when he was clean-shaven.

"You did an exemplary job of wearing me out. My body just has an internal time clock." She slid her leg closer to his and entwined them together. "But it's not like we have to get up yet."

He gave a half-laugh. "My dick needs a break so don't even think about more sex this morning."

"I was thinking more along the lines of a shower."

He groaned. "You know damn well if I get into a shower naked with you, it will not be sex-free."

"What if I promise to keep my hands to myself?" She wiggled her fingers in front of his face.

He grabbed her moving fingers and kissed them, sucking one into his mouth making her moan. "Fine, let's go." He threw the covers off them and picked her up.

"Hey," she shrieked as he carried her to the bathroom, both of them naked. "Put me down."

He did, but not until she stood in the middle of the shower. "You're the one who wanted to take a shower." As he said it he stepped back and turned the water on, cold water cascading down over her.

"I'm gonna kill you!" He was standing outside the shower door, laughing like a crazy person at what he'd done to her.

"You are never getting sex again!" It was an empty threat, but still, she had to say something to make him pay. Turning the water to hot she stood under the spray to warm up.

"Don't make threats you have no intention of keeping," he said from outside the shower. "You love me and there's no taking it back."

Before she could respond the door slid open and he came up behind her nuzzling her neck. "I'm sorry."

She could feel his smile as he spoke the words. "You are not." She turned in his arms. "But I'll forgive you. This time."

Water washed over them as they each ran their hands over the other's body. It was enough just to be in there with him being able to touch him. They didn't need to progress to sex.

They took turns washing each other and exchanging deep, sensual kisses. It was almost like they were in a dream state as their hands roamed their bodies.

When the water turned cold, they finally stepped out, Anthony wrapping her in a big fluffy towel.

"Except for the beginning, that might have been the best shower I've ever taken."

He tied his towel around his waist. "I won't complain if you want to come shower with me every day."

Walking back into his bedroom, she found her bag on the floor where Anthony left it the night before. Grabbing her brush from the side pocket, she began to brush out her hair. "Why does it suck so bad that we can't be together every night? Normal people who start relationships don't spend every night with each other, do they?"

"I think it's hard because, while we just started seeing each other, we have been circling each other for a while. Plus, maybe it's the whole, we can't thing that makes it harder."

"I guess," she said. He was probably right on both points, but she hated to admit it. "At least we had last night and we'll also have all day."

Tonight was her aunt's barbecue and all her friends and family would be there, but so would Anthony. That gave her more time to spend with him.

He'd been dressing but he stopped cold and looked up at her. "You want to spend the whole day with me?"

She grabbed her clothes from her bag. "I assumed we would since we are having breakfast and we have to be at my aunt's at three. I guess we don't have to if you don't want to?"

"No, I want to. I just hadn't thought past breakfast and then the barbecue." He took two steps and landed right in front of her. "I'd love to spend the whole day with you."

She smiled up at him. "Maybe we'll get sick of each other and the whole wanting to be together twenty-four-seven will go away."

He kissed her, just a light graze of his lips against hers. "Perish the thought."

After they were dressed they drove back to Cedarville to meet Reed and Ryan for breakfast at IHOP. Reed was full of stories about Ryan and Addison and all the games they played and the fun they had.

Carly kept up with Reed's stories, but at the same time, was wondering about Addison and what time she'd left. She was hesitant to ask after the way Anthony had been the night before about his sister and Ryan.

But her question was answered when Addison showed up a few minutes later. "Hey guys, I hope it's okay that I'm crashing. Ryan said it would be okay."

"It's fine." Carly pulled out a chair next to her. "Come sit."

Carly was dying to have a moment alone with Addison and she got her chance when they both went to the bathroom at the same time.

"Quick tell me what happened last night?"

Addison looked at her crazily. "What are you talking about?"

"You and Ryan and don't lie and tell me there isn't something there. I have eyes."

She rolled her eyes. "I'm rethinking this having friends thing."

"Seriously," Carly put her hands on her hips. "You can never get rid of me now that I'm in your life. Now give me the details."

"There are no details to give. Am I attracted to him? Umm, yeah. He's hot and funny and sweet with Reed. But am I going to do anything about it? No. He lives in Baltimore. No way in hell am I starting anything long distance. And that only leaves a one night stand and while I'm tempted, I just think it would be bad with you and Ryan needing to see each other because of Reed."

Carly pursed her lips. "Well, that sucks. You guys had some serious vibes."

"You think?"

"Yeah and I'm not the only one who noticed."

"Oh God, Tony could tell?"

"He's the one who first mentioned it, but then he went all caveman and didn't like the idea of you and him."

"That makes me want to sleep with him just to piss him off."

"Oh fuck, please don't. If you do that, he will be all surly and annoyed and it will affect my sex life."

"Right," she snorted. "Like anything could affect you two."

"You're probably right, but he'll still be annoyed and I'll still have to deal with him." After using the restroom, both of them rejoined the rest of their group at the table.

After breakfast, they took Reed to a park to play and interestingly enough, Addison stayed. She could deny it all she wanted, but there was something between her and Ryan.

While Addison and Anthony were swinging with Reed, Carly took a seat on the bench next to Ryan.

"He's really opened up since he's been here," Ryan said, his eyes glued to Reed and what he was doing.

"I think it's this town. Everyone who comes here loves it. We joke that there's something in the water."

He laughed. "It might be true."

She looked over at him. "This might not be any of my business, Ryan, but you seem so stressed."

"I am stressed. My job is non-stop and it seems like everything gets dumped on me." He sighed. "And don't take this the wrong way, but I'm a little jealous of how great a job you are doing with Reed."

"You shouldn't be. It hasn't been all roses and I just happened to be lucky enough to be able to take the time off to be with him. If I didn't own the studio, there is no way I would have been able to do that. Plus, and this is the big one, Reed adores you. He talks about you daily and loves when you FaceTime him. You did everything right, including bringing him to me to help out while you get work done."

"I just feel like a failure. And when I look over there at that happy little boy, I can't help but think I am no better than his parents."

Carly bit her bottom lip wondering if she should say what she was thinking. In the end, she kept her mouth shut. They didn't know each other that well and she didn't want to piss him off with her suggestions that maybe he slow down, find a less stressful job.

Not her place.

"You'll figure it all out," she said instead.

"At least someone has faith in me." He stood and walked over to where Reed was. Once he was there, Anthony came and sat next to her.

"That kid is wearing me out." He turned toward her, picking up her hand in his to hold. She loved how he always wanted to be touching her.

"He does have a lot of energy." She glanced over at him before turning back to Anthony. "You look happy."

He lifted her hand to his mouth and kissed her knuckles. "That's because I get to spend the whole day with my girl."

She rolled her eyes at his cheesiness, even though deep down she secretly loved it. "You're an idiot."

He leaned his body in toward hers, his face almost touching hers. "As long as you love me, I don't care."

She closed the distance and kissed his lips lightly. "I guess you'll do."

They went back to enjoying watching Reed play as they held hands. She couldn't help but think again, that in a few years, this could be their life.

Her Aunt Alice hadn't been kidding when she'd said she bought tons of stuff for kids. When they'd gotten to her house, Reed was so excited, he had a hard time choosing what to do first. The bounce house won out and Carly was pretty sure he stayed in that thing for at least an hour.

Her aunt and uncle took over watching Reed and shooed her and Ryan out of the way, telling them to go enjoy themselves. Since Ryan had already met Leah and Melanie, she introduced him to Logan and Brandon.

"It's nice to meet you," they both said, as they took turns shaking Ryan's hand.

Carly left them alone as they started talking and went to find Leah and Mel. She found them lounging in chairs on the deck along with Addison.

"Ladies," she said as she walked up behind them.

"It's about time," Melanie said. "What took you so long?"

"And please don't tell me you stopped to have sex with my brother?" Addison added. "I do not need to hear about that."

"What do you think we are, a bunch of animals?" She'd be offended, but Addison was halfway right. While they hadn't stopped to have sex, they did have a pretty hot make-out session in her car before they left her house. When Ryan had offered to drive Reed, she hadn't objected in the least.

"If Tony is anything like Brandon, then yes, you two are a bunch of animals," Leah said.

Melanie high fived her. "For real."

Carly found an empty chair and pulled it up to sit with them. "If we are going to pick on people, I think it should be Addison." Carly raised her eyebrows to her new friend. "It seems there is some major chemistry between her and Ryan."

"Shut the front door!" Leah shouted. "Why am I the last to know everything?"

"Hey, I didn't know either," Mel said. "So don't pretend like you were the only one."

Leah swatted her words off with her hand. "Info. Now."

"Do you want to do the honors?" Carly asked, looking toward Addison.

"It's nothing. Seriously. You and Tony just have love on the brain and are seeing things that aren't there."

"Wrong," Carly said. "Stop lying."

She huffed out a breath. "Fine if you must know. Yes, there is something there, but like I told Carly this morning, nothing is going to happen. He lives in Baltimore and a one night stand is out because of Reed."

"Way to deflate my bubble," Mel said. "I thought we were going to get a juicy story."

"There is no juice. I promise."

"Okay," Leah started. "Let's roll this back a minute and pretend he did live here. Then would you act?"

Leave it to Leah to get down to the heart of things.

Addison bit her lip and averted her gaze. "I'm not sure. There is still the whole Reed thing and I wouldn't want to do anything to make it weird."

"I get that," Mel said. "I was worried about that when Logan and I first got together. And while there wasn't a child involved, there was the fact that my best friend was his cousin. That gave me a few moments of pause in the beginning."

"How'd you decide it was worth the chance?"

"When you love someone as much as I love Logan, there was no decision to make. I had to try or I'd have been miserable forever."

"Well, when I fall in love with someone, I promise I will try. But attraction is not love."

"It can turn into it though," Leah said. "Take Bran and me. We had just met and the attraction was through the roof. Once we gave into it, it wasn't long before it became more."

Addison sighed. "Can we be done with this now? I really don't want to think about the fact that the first guy I have been attracted to in years lives hundreds of miles away and is off-limits. It sucks."

Being the awesome friends they were, they changed the subject to puppies and how Melanie and Logan were going to pick one out from the pound the next week. When the guys joined them, including Ryan, but not Anthony, Carly went to look for him. She found him in the living room talking to her dad and his parents. Or who she assumed were his parents.

"Hey, dad," she said, giving him a hug.

"Carly," Anthony said when the hug ended, "I'd like you to meet my parents, Ray and Greta."

"It's nice to see you again, Ray." She shook his hand. "And Greta – awesome name by the way – nice to meet you."

"Happy to be here," his mom beamed. "Aren't you gorgeous."

Carly laughed. "I'm not in Addison's league, so I'm not sure about gorgeous."

"You're one hundred percent gorgeous," Anthony said and pulled her into his side.

PDA hadn't ever been an issue for her. But, for some reason standing in front of her dad and his parents, it felt odd. She tried to break free of his embrace but was only tucked in closer to him.

In her ear he whispered, "Stop trying to get away from me."

She slapped his chest and went back to talking to his parents. "Come on out back and I can introduce you to my aunt and uncle."

"I'll do that, honey," her dad said. "You young people should enjoy your day and let us old folks enjoy having a little one around."

Carly knew better than to try and argue with her dad, so she let them go.

"Why'd you go all tense when I put my arm around you?"

Why did the man have to notice everything? "I just wasn't sure how I felt about being all touchy-feely in front of our parents. Is that weird for you?"

"Carly, I am a grown man. It's not as if my parents think I'm a monk. And honestly, I'm pretty sure they are just happy that I am happy."

"Well, now I feel like an idiot."

"Welcome to the club." He was referring to that morning when she had called him one.

"We might as well go back out to the deck and see what everyone is up to."

"Lead the way."

They found everyone still outside, and from the looks of it, Ryan was fitting right in. She hoped being in Cedarville was helping him loosen up. He was a nice guy, and now that he was part of their group of friends, she was going to try hard to push him into happiness.

Chapter 16

Tony said goodbye to his parents one last time before they finally left the party. They'd had a great time or, at least it'd looked like they had. Reed had fallen asleep over an hour ago in the guest room and Carly was arguing with her aunt about taking him home. She was trying to get her to just let him stay and Carly was unsure. Sidling up next to her, he kept quiet and let her make the decision.

"I'm just not sure," she said. "What if he wakes up and gets scared?"

"Then I'll go in and calm him down."

"But he doesn't know he is staying. Waking up in a strange room could traumatize him."

"I have a suggestion." Tony heard Ryan's voice come up behind them. "What if I stay too?"

Carly furrowed her brow at him. "Why would you do that?"

"Because I kinda agree with your aunt. He's tired and worn out. There is no need to wake him if we don't have to."

"Smart man," Alice said.

Carly let out a breath. "All right. If you guys are cool with it, then I'm on board."

"I'll just run back to your house, Carly and grab my bag and a few things for Reed."

Ryan left the house and Alice went to start cleaning up. Taking her by the elbow, he led Carly to the couch.

"Is this a problem for you?"

"No. Or at least I don't think so. I just worry I've now left him two nights in a row."

"But Ryan will be here and was there last night. It's not as if you are abandoning him."

"I know that in here." She pointed to her head. "But in here," she touched her chest over her heart, "I worry."

"What are you going to do when he goes back to Baltimore with Ryan?" He'd been wanting to ask her that question for days, but a good time had never really come up.

"I'm refusing to think about that." She smiled a very forced smile up at him.

"Maybe you should start thinking about it."

"I can't. Not yet." She turned her body to face him. "Obviously, not dealing with things is a bad trait of mine." She waved a hand around the room. "My mom, ex-douchebag boyfriend, you. I know I suck at it. But I have to do it my way."

He leaned in, face close to hers. "Just do me a favor? Remember you won't be going through it alone."

She searched his eyes. "I can only promise to try."

Lifting a hand to cup her face he kissed her, long and slow. It was a kiss that left them both panting for air when it was over.

"Are you ready to get out of here?"

"That depends," she said. "Are you coming home with me?"

"I thought you'd never ask."

Everyone else was still hanging out on the back deck, but as far as Tony was concerned the party could end that very second and he'd be happy. He was looking forward to another night where he got to spend the whole thing with Carly and then got to wake up with her in his arms. But he didn't want to force her to leave.

Their friends were loud and boisterous when they stepped out onto the deck.

"Carly!" Leah bellowed and everyone turned to look at them.

"Somebody's drunk," Carly said. "Cut her off." She pointed to Brandon.

"Are you kidding?" He raised his eyebrows. "I get laid when she's like this."

"Pretty sure you get laid when she's sober too," Logan said from behind him.

"Yeah, but drunk sex," Brandon shook his head, "that's the best."

"Guys are pigs," Melanie said. "And idiots."

"Yes, but they're cute pigs." Leah stretched up on her toes and kissed Brandon.

Music was playing in the background and all of a sudden it changed to something upbeat and fast tempo.

"Let's dance!" Mel shouted and grabbed both Carly and Addison's hands, pulling them to a corner of the deck. Leah followed and together they sang and danced.

"Looks like Addison is fitting right in with them," Logan said.

Tony looked over at the four women who were dancing and laughing. "It's nice to see her have fun."

He watched them dance for a few minutes before turning back to the guys. "Logan, I'll be ready to start on Monday, if you're good with that?" He'd spent all his free time the last week making the plans for the security install at Logan's Gallery.

"Don't see a reason why not. You've got a key, so come and go as you need to."

"I'm helping out with Reed for a couple of days, so I'll have to cut out early."

"I was wondering what the plan was when she went back to work," Brandon said. "Leah was talking about it but my mind wasn't really listening."

"Did you just admit to not listening to your girlfriend while she was talking?" Logan cocked his head.

"Yeah, but this is like Vegas," he circled his hand around them. "What is said here, stays here."

"Maybe instead of trying to get us to keep your secret, you should just start paying attention when she talks." Tony laughed.

"Yeah well, try paying attention when your girlfriend is stripping naked in the living room while she's telling you a story. I promise you, it is not possible."

"Please tell me you didn't have sex on your couch." Logan shivered. "I'm never going to be able to sit there again."

"I suggest you don't eat at the kitchen table then either."

"Fuck, man." Logan shook his head.

"You're telling me it's safe to sit everywhere at your house?"

Logan cringed and hung his head.

"That's what I thought."

Tony was laughing at their conversation, glad that neither one was asking about his sexual exploits with Carly. The music changed and each girl came wandering back over.

"I hate to be a party pooper," Addison said, "but I think I'm gonna head home."

"Are you driving?" Tony asked, unsure of how much she'd had to drink.

"Even though I've been drinking water for two hours, I called a cab."

"We're heading out too," Brandon said, pulling Leah firmly into his side.

The rest of them all agreed and followed them to the front of the house. Once Addison's cab had arrived and the other's had driven away, he and Carly headed to her house. She'd had more to drink than him, so Tony drove her car.

"I'm exhausted," she dropped her head back against the headrest. "This day has really worn me out."

He looked over at her and saw her eyes closed on her tired face. "We'll be home soon and you can fall asleep."

"Uh uh," she shook her head. "Do you actually think I am going to waste my time with you sleeping?"

"Yes, I do. You need your sleep and I am not going to be the reason you don't get it."

She opened her eyes and looked at him. "What'd I ever do to deserve you?"

He let out a half-laugh, half choke. "I'm pretty sure it's the other way around."

"You're joking, right?" She sat forward. "My life is this crazy soap opera and you're over there all perfect and shit, asking how you can help. That doesn't happen in real life."

He pulled into her driveway, and parked next to his truck. Shutting off the engine he turned to her. "Love doesn't care about things like unexpected brothers showing up or mom's who treated their kids badly. Love just is. And, in my limited experience with it, there's no turning back or flipping a switch. You either love someone or you don't. Crazy soap opera life or not."

Silence settled in around them. "Thank you for a great day."

He took her hand across the console. "I love you."

"I love you too."

Tony woke when he felt the covers move from his body and the bed dip at his hips. He didn't open his eyes for fear that Carly would stop what he thought she was getting ready to do.

He was rewarded seconds later when her warm mouth engulfed his erect cock. He stayed as still as possible while she teased and tormented him with her skilled tongue and mouth. After several minutes it became impossible for him to hold still. Opening his eyes he found her looking up at him through hooded lashes.

Resting his hands on her head, he guided her head as her mouth continued its wicked ways. When he could no longer hold his pleasure back, he lifted his head and watched as he came. His eyes were glued to where her mouth was connected to his dick as she swallowed every drop that came from him. When he could look no longer, for fear he'd be hard again in seconds, he flopped back against the bed.

Breathing heavy, he closed his eyes and tried to get his body under control. How was it that he was still hard and ready to take her? He was a thirty-five-year-old man. It wasn't supposed to be like this, was it?

"Good morning." She snuggled back up next to him, her hair splaying across his chest.

"Great morning," he said, his voice gravelly.

"That was a thank you for being amazing this whole weekend."

He looked down at her, lifting her chin up with his fingers so she'd have to look at him. "I don't need a thank you for spending time with you. I spend time with you because not spending time with you is torture. If I had to choose between watching you clean toilets or, I don't know, anything else, I'd choose to watch you clean toilets. I'd always choose you."

She grinned. "Now I feel like I need to thank you again."

He knew she was kidding but went along with it anyway. "I'd be game." He rolled them both so he was on top of her.

"Aren't you like old?" Her eyes were lit with humor. "How do you recover so fast?"

He dipped his head and nipped her ear. "Did you just call me old?"

He felt her shiver under him from his kiss to her ear. "I'm just sayin'. I thought you old guys needed more time to...get it up again."

"You're going to pay for that."

"Ohhh, I'm scared," she teased.

Sitting up onto his knees, he rolled her so she was on her stomach. Tilting her hips only a little, he lined up and entered her in one swift move.

"Holy shit," she said, her voice muffled by the pillow.

"You're going to feel me so deep inside of you like this." He kissed down her spine. He began moving slowly in and out, loving her moans. As he got deeper she got louder until soon she was cursing and shouting into the bed.

"Oh yeah, that's it. You feel so fucking good." She wasn't shy and he loved how vocal she was when they made love.

"You're fucking gorgeous like this. Your ass is sexy as hell." He cupped it in his hands and kneaded her flesh. He slowed his strokes, driving them both insane with pleasure. When his knees began to hurt, he rolled them both on their sides, never disconnecting their bodies. In this position he was just as deep but now he had access to her tits. All was right in the world.

Losing track of time, they made unhurried, steady love. There was no rushing. No dash to climax. It was just the two of them, enjoying the feel of each other's bodies. When he couldn't take it any longer, he accelerated his speed. When her breathing changed, he went just a little faster and deeper, hoping he could hold off long enough for her to come first.

She half-turned toward him, pulling his head down to hers for a kiss. He knew from experience that this was a sign she was almost there. A few more thrusts and sure enough, her body shook and she tightened around his cock. Once he felt that, he let himself go and came with her.

With his body exhausted from their lovemaking, he stayed just where he was. Sleeping like this, with their bodies still connected would be totally okay with him. Unfortunately though, it was morning and soon Reed would be home.

"I guess being old has its advantages," she said languidly.

He laughed. "That'll teach you to call me old." He gave her one last kiss before retreating from her bed to go clean up. In the bathroom, he found a clean washcloth under the sink and dampened it with warm water. Strolling back into her room, he used the damp cloth to wash between her legs.

"God, I wish I could lie in bed all day." She sighed and sat up. "I feel like I am being pulled in a million different directions. And it sucks because I want to do them all."

"It's going to get easier." He found his pants on the floor and pulled them on. "You'll get into a rhythm and everything will be fine."

"I'll get into a rhythm and then Reed will leave."

He sat on the bed. "It's not like you'll never see him again. You're part of his life now."

She pressed the heels of her hands to her eyes. "I'm not thinking about that. I'm going to enjoy him while I have him, and deal with everything else later." She stood. "I'm gonna take a quick shower."

He leaned back against the bed to think. He knew deep down she was going to be hurt and miserable once the month was up and Reed went back to Baltimore with Ryan. Her refusal to deal with it before it happened was not the way to go. But it wasn't his place to tell her how to feel or act.

She'd have to get there on her own.

Chapter 17

After two straight days of non-stop activity, Carly was glad to finally sit down and relax. Ryan had just left and Reed was settled in her bed watching a movie while she tried to stay awake. It was only seven, but to her it felt more like midnight. Reed wanted to show Ryan everything. And when he'd said everything. He'd meant it.

They'd gone all over town, stopping at every place Reed wanted to show Ryan. Then they had a quick early dinner so Ryan could get on the road back to Baltimore.

The only bad part about her day was that Anthony hadn't joined them. He'd told her he had work to do but she'd known it was a lie. She wasn't sure why he lied and why he didn't want to spend the day with them, but she'd been in no mood to question his motives.

He was a grown man and he could either speak up or not. It wasn't her problem.

Except, it felt like it was her problem; like he was her problem. And the funny thing was, she wanted it to be her problem.

Leaning her head back she looked toward Reed. He'd fallen asleep somewhere along the way and now dozed peacefully in her bed. Standing up, she went to the other side of the bed and picked him up in her arms. He stirred but didn't fully wake. Carrying him to his room, she covered him with his blanket and kissed his head.

"Night buddy."

She left his door open and walked downstairs to get some water. She'd just turned on the light in the kitchen, when she heard a light knock on her door. She knew, without even looking, who it would be and when she opened the door, sure enough, there stood Anthony.

"Hey," he said. "I hope I'm not interrupting?"

She held the door open. "Come in," she said in a clipped tone.

She closed the door behind him but didn't follow him into her living room. "What are you doing here?"

"I wanted to explain…about this morning and not spending the day with you."

"I'm not mad if that's what you think." That was partly a lie. She was mad but she couldn't figure out why.

"Could have fooled me."

"Dammit, Tony." She threw her hands in the air.

"You called me Tony." His eyes went wide. "You never call me Tony?"

"I know and I don't know why," she practically shouted. "Maybe I am mad."

His demeanor never changed and he didn't seem upset or angry. "The only reason I didn't come with you today was I thought you needed time alone with Reed. I didn't want to be in the way."

She huffed out a breath. "You wouldn't have been in the way. Reed loves spending time with you."

"And I love spending time with him but –" He stopped and his fingers rubbed his facial hair on his chin. "I just wanted you to have as much time with him as possible without me around."

She sat down next to him. She couldn't fault him for thinking of her but she wanted him to know he didn't always have to. "Let me ask you something. Was the only reason you didn't spend the day with us because you were thinking of me and what I needed?"

He shrugged. "Yeah."

She moved closer to him. "What about you? What did you want to do?"

"I wanted to be with you. And Reed."

She laid her hand on his leg. "In doing something you thought I needed you missed out on doing something you wanted. You shouldn't have to do that."

"I guess I didn't think about it like that."

"I wish you would. Because I don't want to be the reason you miss out on doing things that you want."

He looked down to where her hand was touching him. Threading his own fingers through hers, he lifted their joined hands. "It's hard for me to think about myself when it's so much more important to me that you are happy."

"Don't you think I feel the same way?" She tilted her head to the side. "Can't we both be happy?"

"If I promise to start taking myself into consideration, will you promise to talk to me when I do something that bothers you? I could tell you didn't understand this morning and I kept waiting for you to ask. But you never did."

"It's a bad habit I have...thinking the worst. But I promise to try and do better."

He leaned in and kissed her. "That's all I ask."

She lifted her free hand and ran it through his hair. "Tell me about your day?"

"I spent most of it at Logan's gallery making sure measurements were correct. It was pretty boring unless you count Logan and Melanie arguing."

"They always do that. I actually think it's worse now that they are together."

"It's amusing, that's for sure. What about your day?"

She dropped her head back. "It was exhausting. Reed wanted to show Ryan everything. That entailed going all over town. While some we drove to, a lot of the time we walked."

"Sounds like a fun day. I'm sorry I was an idiot and missed it."

"You won't hear a disagreement from me on the idiot part, but I am sorry you missed it." She studied him. He hadn't shaved in several days and his scruff was a real turn on. "Maybe you can make it up to me by staying tonight?"

He narrowed his eyes. "What about Reed?"

"When Ryan left, the last thing he said to me was that he didn't see it being a problem if you were to ever stay over. He said that if it were him, and he knew the person he was with was going to be in his life for the long haul, then he wouldn't see a problem with overnights."

He smiled. "Are we in it for the long haul?"

She rolled her eyes at him. "Don't be an ass. You know how I feel about you."

"And how do you feel about me?"

She bit her bottom lip. "I love you, you big idiot."

He leaned into her, resting his forehead against hers. "I love you too. And, for the record, I would love to stay over."

"Would it be horrible if I said it would just be for sleep? I'm freaking exhausted, and to be honest, I'm having a hard time keeping my eyes open."

He stood, lifting her with him. "Considering you almost killed me this morning, I think sleep is a good idea."

"Me?" she scoffed. "You were the one who had to have a marathon sex session. I would have been fine with a quickie."

He looked down at her with his eyebrow raised. "You're saying you didn't like it?"

She tried to hold back her smile but it was impossible. "You damn well know how much I liked it. So don't even pretend you don't."

They both laughed. "Do what you need to down here and I'll run out and grab my bag."

She watched him walk out the door, his jeans molded perfectly to his ass, and, damn, the man had a nice ass.

The next morning, she dropped Reed off to school and went to the studio to teach. She was early and thought for sure she'd be the first person there but, lo and behold, both Mel and Leah were there.

"Do you two hate your homes and boyfriends so much that you want to spend all your time here?" She walked by them, dropping her bag on her desk.

"Har har," Leah said. "No dummy, we wanted to be here to welcome you back."

"And we brought donuts!" Mel shouted, holding up a box from the bakery.

"Just what my ass needs."

"Yeah, like that's even an issue," Leah said. "At least you two dance every day. The only activity I get is sex with Brandon."

"If it's anything like sex with Logan, then I am sure you are getting a workout."

"Lalalala, I am not listening to this." Carly had her fingers in her ears.

Mel pulled on her arms, her fingers popping out of her ears. "Get the fuck over it already. We," she indicated between herself and Leah, "are sleeping with your cousins. And we have sex, lots of it. So deal and stop acting like a baby."

Carly narrowed her eyes in a death stare. "You don't get to tell me how to feel."

"In this case, I do." Mel was not backing down. "I want to be able to talk to my friend about my life. My whole life, including sex. So get over it and be my friend."

Carly hated when Mel was right, and this was one of those times. "Fine, but feel free to leave certain things out."

Leah stepped between them. "Now that you two are done arguing, maybe we can enjoy our donuts and talk?"

Grabbing a donut, Carly sat. "Anything I need to know about what's going on here?" Leah had been sending her daily updates on her classes and enrollment info so she stayed up-to-date.

"Nope. I've sent you everything."

"I can't thank you guys enough for covering and taking over last week. I really needed to be there for Reed."

"We've always got your back," Melanie said. "You'd do the same for us."

She would. That's the kind of friendship they had. "What else is going on?"

Leah shrugged. "Same old stuff. Bran has been spending most of his free time helping Logan with the gallery. And since I'm no good at manual labor, I've been helping Alice with the business side. She knows a ton, but needed to be brought up to speed."

"I'm sorry I haven't been around to help much. Is the opening still set for November?"

"Logan thinks so," Melanie said. "He's debating pushing it back another week to have a little extra time."

"Might not be a bad idea," Leah said. "There's still a lot to do and, I know he has a month, but why be rushed if you don't have to."

"I'm with Leah," Carly added. "Remember how rushed we were with this place? That was no fun."

"Let's just hope the crazy shit that went down on our opening day, won't happen with Logan." Mel was referring to her being knocked out by Leah's stalker.

"If you think about it though, that day is the day that changed everything for all of us. Brandon and I became closer, leading us to fall in love. Logan realized you were the one for him after you'd been hurt. And because of Mel being hurt, Logan and Brandon hired Tony to install the security system at the house."

Carly had never connected the dots but Leah was right. "Holy shit! How did I not notice that?"

"That's just what I was thinking," Mel said.

"We were all busy," Leah said. "The only reason I thought of it was that, on Saturday, Addison was asking me how we all met each other. And when I got to how we all met our guys, it kinda hit me how important that day was."

"A few weeks ago, I would have said meeting Anthony that day was not a good thing. Now...well let's just say, it's amazing what a few weeks will do."

"You are ridiculously cute together," Melanie said. "He's always touching you."

"I noticed that too," Leah said. "You're like his lifeline."

Funny, she had thought the same thing about him. "Is he really? I don't think I ever noticed."

"Of course you didn't notice," Leah said. "We don't notice things if we like them. At least I don't."

"I guess." She shrugged and took a sip of her coffee. "We kinda fought last night."

"What'd you fight about?" Leah stood up and grabbed another donut.

"Yesterday he said he couldn't come with Ryan, Reed and me, because he had to work. I knew the moment he said it that it was a lie, but I didn't confront him. I let the whole day go by and didn't text or call him. After I put Reed to sleep, he showed up at the house to talk. He'd known I was mad and was angry himself that I didn't speak up."

"Okay," Mel said, "I get that, but did he say why he didn't want to go with you yesterday?"

"His reason was he wanted me to have time with Reed without interfering. It was a legit reason and I get why he did it, but even after we talked about it, I still kinda feel like there was maybe another reason?"

She wasn't able to put her finger on it, but something in his eyes and voice had led her to believe he wasn't being one hundred percent honest.

"Did you ask him?" Mel was using her scolding voice.

"I felt stupid asking him. We had just dealt with it and his reason made sense. I had nothing to go on."

"Except your gut," Leah said. "Word of advice...don't not say things because you are afraid. It will get you nowhere."

"He's said virtually the same thing to me several times." She dropped her head back against her chair. "Being in love is a lot of work."

"Tell me about it," Mel laughed. "I love, love, love Logan, but boys are idiots. I feel like I am always fixing his problems."

"Bran is just as bad. How that man can be in charge of protecting the whole town, but can't figure out where to put the cups in the dishwasher, is beyond me."

Carly laughed knowing her friends were joking to try and make her feel better. "So it's not just Tony, they're all like that?"

"Yep," Leah said. "They're all like that."

They all laughed. Carly picked up her bag and stood. "I'm gonna head into the studio now and get myself ready to teach. It's been a whole week, after all."

Entering what had become her studio, she put her stuff away then turned on the music. She needed a few minutes to loosen up her body after a week off. After a few stretches she began to dance. It wasn't amazing or fancy, it was just her. While she danced she tried to clear her mind of all her insecurities and just let go.

It wasn't easy but she did it. And when she was finished, she felt refreshed and ready to tackle anything and everything life could throw at her.

Chapter 18

Luckily for Tony, he was working at Logan's gallery in Cedarville and it was only a short drive to Reed's elementary school. School let out at four and Tony knew he was cutting it close, but he'd gotten caught up in the install and pushed it too far.

When he pulled up to the school with four minutes to spare, relief washed over him. He, in no way, wanted to let Reed—or Carly, for that matter—down. Cars were lined up along the sidewalk just like Carly said they would be and when he heard the bell ring, kids upon kids came rushing out of the school. He got out of his truck and stood next to it so Reed would be sure to see him. He spotted him after only a few minutes and when Reed didn't seem to notice him, he waved his arm and shouted, "Reed, over here!"

Reed turned his head and ran toward him, plowing full force into him with a hug. "Tony, guess what, I made a new friend. His name is Danny, and him and I both love dinosaurs."

"Wow buddy, that's awesome." Tony reluctantly pulled away from the hug, floored by his easy show of affection. "Jump on in and you and I will head home." He opened the door and made sure Reed was in his booster seat safely with the seat belt latched,before he went around to his side.

"So, whatcha wanna do tonight?" He started the car and pulled out.

Reed was quiet and when Tony glanced over at him, his head was turned away. "Are you okay?"

"Do you think Carly misses Max?"

It was an odd question, and it threw Tony for a loop. He knew Max was still at Carly's dad's house because Reed was afraid of dogs. "I'm sure she misses him, but I know for a fact he loves spending time where he is."

"But wouldn't he like being at his home more?" His small voice held so much emotion.

"Probably." He phrased his next question carefully. "Have you ever had a dog?"

Had Tony not turned his head to look at him, he never would have seen the shiver of the boy's body.

"No, but my neighbors used to, and they were mean."

"How do you know they were mean?" He wasn't sure if he wanted an answer to the question, even though he'd asked it.

"They used to fight. The dogs."

"Sometimes that happens. Dogs get mad just like people."

"They did it on purpose. The people wouldn't feed them and then they'd put them in cages together."

Fuck. Reed was talking about dog fights and not only was that cruel to animals, it was cruel for a little boy to see. That must have been what made him terrified of dogs. Hell, Tony was a grown man and that might've had an effect on him.

Tony was almost to Carly's, but he felt like he needed to stop so Reed and he could talk this out. So he pulled over into an empty lot.

"I bet that was scary, seeing dogs fight like that."

"I didn't like it. Sometimes my dad would go and make me go with him."

For about the hundredth time, Tony wanted to kill that bastard and thanked God he was already dead. "You know not everyone does that right? Most people feed their dogs and teach them not to fight?"

He shrugged but stayed silent. Tony was out of his depth and wondered why Reed had chosen him to tell this story.

He was just about to say something when Reed said, "Maybe I can meet Max?"

At that moment, when a six-year-old boy who was deathly afraid of dogs, decided he wanted to face his fear, Tony fell in love for the second time in his life.

"You know it's okay to be afraid of things, right?" He wanted this brave boy to know that being afraid did not make him less of a person.

"Have you met Max? Is he nice?"

"He's a big, lazy bum," Tony laughed. "Sometimes I wonder if he is actually alive."

Reed's eyes went from wary to curious. "So maybe you can take me to meet him, and if I like him, he can come back home? Wouldn't that make Carly happy?"

And then Tony understood. Reed was doing this for Carly, and hell, he couldn't blame the kid, because he himself would do anything for the woman. "She's okay with Max staying with her dad. She doesn't want you to be afraid."

"I don't want to be afraid either."

His voice sounded like there might be tears and Tony's heart almost broke. He wasn't a dad, and Reed wasn't his kid, so he had no idea what the right thing to do was. But, he had to go with his instinct.

"I'll make you a deal. We will go by and see Max. After you see him, if you decide you'd like to maybe pet him, then you can. But if you don't, that's okay too."

Reed gave him a nod. Tony started the truck and pulled back out on the road. He didn't have Carly's dad's number to call ahead, so he just drove straight there. When he pulled up, Mike happened to be outside. Stepping from his truck, he quickly filled Mike in before Reed got out of the truck and joined them.

"I hear you want to check out Max?" Mike said.

"Is he nice?" his small voice said. "Do you think he'll like me?"

"I think he'll love you." Mike put his hand on Reed's shoulder and steered him toward the backyard, stopping at the gate. "You guys stay right here and I will go get Max."

Tony crouched down to be level with Reed. "Remember, if you see him and then decide you don't want to pet him, we can go."

Mike was holding Max by his collar as they walked up next to the fence. Max was moving slowly like he always did, with a look on his face that said he'd rather be napping. When he saw Tony and Reed, his ears perked up, but only a little. He really was the laziest dog. Sticking his nose through the fence, he sniffed and Tony reached out a hand to pet his nose.

"He's big," Reed said, but his voice didn't sound afraid.

"He is big," Mike said from above them, "but he's a giant baby."

Tony was still petting his nose and letting Max lick him. "What do you think?"

"Does his tongue feel funny?" Reed's eyes were big as he watched Max licking him.

"Not funny, but it is a little rough." Tony looked up to Mike and then asked, "Do you want to let him smell you?"

Reed lifted his hand a little and then stopped. "Are you sure he won't bite?"

"Max doesn't have enough energy to bite anyone," Mike said.

Reed looked at Tony, his face unsure. "I promise you, buddy, I won't let anything happen to you." After he said the words, he knew without a doubt, they were true.

Lifting his hand further, it was finally right under Max's nose. First, Max sniffed it and then he began licking it, same as he'd done to Tony.

"It tickles." Reed was giggling at the feel of the dog's tongue. "But it doesn't hurt."

Tony watched as Reed got braver and took a step closer to the fence. With his other hand he touched the top of Max's nose. "He's soft."

"If you think his nose is soft, you should feel the rest of him," Mike said.

Reed looked at Tony. "Are you sure he won't hurt me?"

"Promise." He held out his pinky as he and his friends did as kids. "Pinky swear." Reed did the same and they hooked their pinkies together.

"Step back and I'll bring Max out," Mike said. As he opened the gate, Tony and Reed took two steps backward. Mike had a firm grip on Max's collar, so there was no way he was going to knock Reed over.

"Take your time," Tony said as he reached out his own hand and stroked Max's head. Tentatively, Reed did the same. And, after a couple of pats to his head, Reed moved closer, this time petting his back.

"He really is soft," Reed said, his voice in awe. "And I think he likes me."

"I think he does too," Tony agreed. Max chose that moment to lie down at Reed's feet. "I told you he was lazy."

Reed laughed and sat down too. He never stopped petting Max, the dog loving the attention.

Tony stood and looked at Mike. "Looks like Max has a new friend." They stood and watched Reed pet Max for more than five minutes. All of Reed's fear had gone out the door as soon as he'd met Max, and Tony was glad he had been there to witness the monumental event.

Reed looked up at him and asked, "Do you think we can take Max back home with us?"

Before he could answer, Mike spoke up, "I think both Max and Carly would love that. Not to mention, I think now that he's met you, Max would miss you."

"Ya think?" Reed said.

"I do. I'll go grab his stuff so you guys can get him home."

After Mike walked away, Tony sat down in the grass next to Reed and Max. "Are you okay with this?"

Reed looked up at him. "I think Max really wants to go home and he's not mean at all."

"You're a pretty amazing kid. I'm glad I met you." Together they stood and began walking to the truck. Max lazily followed along. After they'd loaded up his things, and then helped him into the back seat, they headed home.

Well, home for Max and Reed.

Dinner with a six-year-old and a dog that decided said six-year-old was his new best friend, was an event. Reed had decided Max didn't like dog food and people food would be a better fit. That led to a discussion that some people food is not good for dogs which led to Reed asking why about four hundred times.

Tony might have underestimated how much work taking care of a kid was.

By the time dinner was over, Reed was snuggled up on the couch using Max as a pillow. Before they could move, Tony pulled his phone from his pocket and snapped a pic.

Carly finally walked in the door a little after eight and stopped in her tracks when she saw Max.

"What's going on? Why is Max here?" Because Reed was already in bed, she didn't know how close the two had become.

"Come in, relax, and I will explain."

"But Reed is afraid of dogs." There was panic in her voice.

"He was afraid of dogs. Not so much anymore. At least, he's not afraid of Max."

"Okay, I think I've obviously missed something." She finally dropped her bag and sat down onto the couch with Max. "Hey boy, mom's missed you." She kissed his head.

Tony told her the whole story about how Max came to be back at home. Then he showed her the picture he'd taken of Reed and Max on his phone.

"He really isn't afraid anymore?" she said, eyes glued to the picture on the phone.

"Doesn't seem like it. He even tried to get me to let Max sleep with him."

She shook her head. "That whole story...my mom and Rob were horrible parents. Letting that sweet boy see and hear dog fights."

"He's amazingly well adjusted for all the shit he's probably been through. I mean you should have seen him when he decided to touch Max. He was so fucking brave."

"Thank you for being there with him and for knowing just the right thing to do."

"I was scared out of my mind I was doing the wrong thing and that Max – who I know would never hurt anyone – would suddenly decide to bite."

She scooted closer to him on the couch. "That you did it even though you were scared makes me love you more than I already do."

He reached out to pull her next to him. "Yeah? How much more?"

"Enough that I will..." she paused and moved back, sliding her feet into his lap, "Let you give me a foot massage."

He laughed but took one foot into his hands. "That's a pretty sweet deal."

She moaned when he pressed his fingers into her arch. "Oh God, that feels good. Who knew not dancing for a week would make me so sore."

He kept up the foot rub as they talked about their days. She told him about all her classes and the students and he told her about the job at Logan's and the rest of the night with Reed. When she began to doze off, he woke her up.

"Hey," he said, leaning over her and kissing her lips lightly, "Why don't you head up to bed. You're worn out."

Wrapping her arms around his neck and pulling him in for another kiss, she asked, "Are you coming with me to bed?" Her voice was sleepy and sexy.

"I think I should go home." He didn't want to go home, but he also didn't want to overstay his welcome.

"Stay. Please." She was peppering kisses all over his face and playing with his hair at the base of his neck. He was so turned on from just those two things that leaving had just become impossible.

"Come on, sleepy. Let's get you upstairs." He lifted her into his arms and carried her up the stairs before depositing her in her bed. He went back downstairs to lock up and, when he re-entered the room, she was fast asleep. He stood and just watched her sleep. To him, she was gorgeous, but his love for her was about so much more. She was generous and had a huge heart which was something so many people had given up on in life.

For a second, he debated leaving and going home to his own house. But, there was nothing there for him. Everything he wanted was at Carly's.

Stripping his clothes off, he slid into bed next to Carly and pulled the covers up over them both.

Sleep came fast whenever he held her in his arms.

Chapter 19

Three weeks flew by and before Carly knew it, she was down to her last night with Reed. She and Ryan had made a plan that he would fly in Friday night, and then Saturday morning, he and Reed would fly back to Baltimore. Friday night was going to be just her and Ryan spending time with Reed and helping him understand everything that was going on.

He knew, as much as a six-year-old could, that he was going back with Ryan. But what they hadn't decided was when he would be back to see Carly or when Carly would go visit him.

Carly had pushed all emotions about Reed leaving to the back of her mind. She didn't want Reed to see her upset or unhappy. It didn't matter to her that she wasn't dealing with her own emotions. She could deal with those when he was gone.

Anthony had said his goodbyes to Reed the previous night, since he wouldn't be seeing him again. Reed had seemed fine and either didn't get it, which she didn't think was true because he seemed so grown up for his age, or, he was doing what she was doing, and hiding his feelings.

She had also been confused by the easy way Anthony had said goodbye to Reed. They'd spent a lot of time together in the month Reed had been there, and they'd become close. So close, that Reed was always telling Anthony things about his childhood.

She wasn't bothered by Reed's choice of confidant, not really. She was glad he felt safe enough with someone to open up. She just wished it was her.

The doorbell rang, and Carly, knowing it was Ryan, yelled, "Come in!" Ryan opened the door, looking more ragged than she'd ever seen him.

"You look like shit." She finished picking up her living room and stood, hands on her hips.

"Thanks for stating the obvious." He set his bag down and practically collapsed on her couch.

She sat down next to him. "Is everything okay?" While he talked to Reed most nights, he'd been vague with her on how he was doing.

He closed his eyes and dropped his head back against the couch. "Have you ever worked toward something for so long because it's what you wanted, but then, once you were within arms reach of it, you realized it's not really what you want anymore?"

"No, but I do know people who have. Melanie, Leah, and Logan have all been in that same situation. What is it you thought you wanted?"

"I thought I wanted this promotion. I was sure it was the thing that was going to make me happy."

"Choosing our paths in life is one of the hardest things we do. I can't tell you what to do or how to choose. The only thing I can say, is listen to your heart and not just your head. Most of the time our heads mess us up."

He turned his head and looked at her. "I'm trying." He let out a deep breath. "So where's Reed?"

"He's out back playing with Max." She stood. "I was just out there but need to check on him again. Why don't you come too?"

Standing he rolled his shoulders. "Lead the way."

Max and Reed were doing the same thing they'd been doing when she'd checked in on them the last time, rolling around on the grass together. While it was evident Reed loved Max, it was just as noticeable how much the dog loved the boy. He whined if Reed wasn't home and slept on his bed until he came back. When Reed walked in the door, Max, who barely moved if he didn't have to, would jump up with enthusiasm.

As soon as Reed saw Ryan, he ran toward him jumping in his arms. "You gotta come meet Max!" Reed pulled him into the yard where Ryan was forced to the ground to pet the dog.

Minutes later, all three of them joined her on the deck where Max sat at Reed's feet.

Ryan looked over at her and she knew this was as good as time as any to talk to Reed about him leaving.

"Reed, do you remember how when I brought you to live with Carly, we talked about it only being for a little while?" Reed looked up at Ryan and nodded. "Well, now it's time to go back home with me."

Carly kept quiet and watched Reed's reaction. "Tonight?" he asked.

"Not tonight, buddy, but tomorrow morning."

Reed looked over to Carly. "Are you coming too?"

She smiled, even though it was a fake smile. "I can't, Reed. I have my job so I have to stay here. Remember, we talked about this?"

"But why can't you come?" He looked at Ryan. "Why can't she come?"

"She lives here, in Cedarville. She can come visit but she can't live in Baltimore."

"What about Max?" Reed looked down to his feet where Max was already snoring.

Ryan looked at her again with a 'what do I say' face. She had no idea what to say or do. She'd known this was going to be hard, but for the last week she'd been talking to Reed about it, and he'd seemed fine.

"Max has to stay here too," Ryan said.

"But he'll miss me if he can't play with me."

"I know, but he's Carly's dog and this is his home."

"Why can't it be my home?" There were tears in his eyes and Carly could hear his little voice crack. "I don't wanna leave!" He ran into the house, Max following him.

Ryan stood to go after him, but Carly put her hand on his arm to stop him. "Let him go." Reluctantly, he sat back down.

"He hates us." He rubbed his hands through his hair.

Carly agreed, but she also knew kids threw tantrums. It was the way of the world. "He won't hate us forever. At some point, he'll get older and realize we did the very best we could."

"Like Rob did? Or your mom?" He stood again and paced on her deck. "He's already had a shit childhood and all we are doing is making it worse."

"What do you suggest we do? We live in two different cities, in two different states. All we can do is love him and care for him. There is nothing else."

He stopped pacing and stood with his back to her, looking out into the yard. "I'm not sure, Carly. Sometimes people need more." He walked away, going back into the house, leaving her alone on the deck.

What was he trying to say? She didn't know how they could give Reed anymore. They were both already doing everything to make sure he had a good, happy life. That was way more than her mom and Rob had ever done. They'd brought a child into the world and then neglected him in the worst way. Ryan and Carly were already better at taking care of Reed than his actual parents.

Granted, the bar was set low with those two.

Not getting anywhere, she went inside to find Ryan and Reed, only the living room was empty. Taking the stairs two at a time, she found Reed in his bed, snuggled up with Max.

Sitting on the side of his bed, she stroked his hair. "I know you're mad and I know this sucks, but Ryan and I are doing everything we can."

He didn't answer but she heard him sniff back his tears. "I'll be here whenever you want to talk and I can come to visit you just like you can come to visit me."

He rolled to his back and looked up at her. "What about Max? Can he come visit me?"

"Maybe," she said. "He does love to ride in cars so a road trip might be fun." She smiled hoping to lighten the mood. Instead he rolled back over and hugged Max.

Figuring he just needed time to adjust, she left his room to go in search of Ryan. When she didn't find him, she looked out the front door of her house and found his rental car was not in the driveway. Picking up her phone, she planned to text him to make sure he was okay, but instead she found a text from him.

Ryan:

I just need some time alone. I'll be back.

Carly:

I know this sucks and I know you have a lot on your plate, but I am here to help as much as I can.

Setting her phone down, she stood in place. She didn't know what to do or how to proceed. She knew what she wanted to do. She wanted to call Anthony. He was her happy place, the one person who calmed her. But she also wanted to deal with this on her own.

What did it say about her that she wanted to lean on someone else all the time?

No, she was not going to call him, she was going to handle her emotions and deal with all the issues herself. She could do this. Before Anthony, she wouldn't have had anyone to lean on.

It was always her and her alone.

She could do this. She hoped.

After a restless night of sleep, Carly woke up early to make Reed and Ryan a big breakfast before they had to take off. She'd heard Ryan come home around midnight but, while she wondered where in the world he had been for six hours, it wasn't her place to ask. She knew what it felt like to be overwhelmed and need space.

She was halfway through her first cup of coffee when Ryan appeared downstairs.

"Morning," she said.

He moved into the kitchen and poured himself a cup of coffee. "Sorry about last night. I just couldn't deal."

"You don't have to apologize to me. We all need to take a break sometimes."

He sat down at the counter. "Yeah, but abandoning Reed like that…I won't be able to do that once we are back in Baltimore."

"Even better that you got it out of your system now." She leaned her hip against the counter. "I'm not an expert, Ryan, but I do know that all parents get overwhelmed and need a break. You're going to have to find a way to do that once you have him full-time, or else you'll explode."

"I'm working on it. It's never been easy for me to open up and relax, but I'm going to try."

"Trying is all you can do. Now, how about some breakfast?"

"Can I help?"

"Nope. You enjoy your coffee." She got busy mixing pancake batter and frying bacon. When she was almost finished, she asked Ryan if he'd go wake Reed. She was nervous about how he'd be in the light of day, but there was nothing she could do about it. He was leaving, and that was that.

She plated the food just as she heard them come down the stairs. "Good morning. I hope you're hungry."

"Starved," Ryan said.

Reed was quiet all through breakfast. Both she and Ryan tried to talk to him, but eventually gave up and talked to each other. They discussed the school Reed was enrolled in and the sitter he got for after school until he'd be home from work. They also made plans for her to come up for Thanksgiving week. The studio was closed the whole week, and that would give her lots of time to spend with Reed.

When breakfast ended, Ryan went to get Reed ready while she cleaned up the kitchen. She'd packed his bags the previous day, so he was all ready to go. All that was left to do was say goodbye to him. They came back downstairs, Reed looking sadder than she'd ever seen him.

Crouching down, she opened her arms. "Can I get a goodbye hug?"

His bottom lip quivered but he ran forward into her arms. "Why do I have to go?"

She hugged him tightly. "You just do. But, I promise, we can talk anytime you want."

"Can you let Max sleep with you? He's gonna be lonely when I'm not here."

"He can sleep with me anytime he wants."

Reed let go and stepped back and looked up to Ryan. "I'm ready." He walked to the door, Max hot on his heels.

"Well, I guess we are leaving," Ryan said. "Thank you. For everything."

Carly's eyes were burning with the need to cry but she stayed strong. "It was my pleasure. Call if you need anything." She gave him a quick hug. "And let me know once you land."

Ryan picked up Reed's bag and together they walked out the front door. Carly walked to the doorway and waved goodbye. Once the car was out of sight, she closed the door. As she started to take a step away, her body gave out and she slid to the floor.

The tears she'd worked so hard to hold back came rushing out. There was no controlling them. Since the day Reed had come to stay with her, she'd known this day would come. And, because she was an idiot, she'd chosen not to deal with it or, even think about it.

Instead she'd fallen in love with a little boy. A little boy who wasn't hers and would never be hers. He lived in Baltimore with Ryan and her home would only ever be for visiting.

She would go back to being alone and there was nothing she could do about it.

The crying turned to dry heaving when there were no more tears to shed. At some point she moved to the couch, Max following and settling in next to her. She heard her phone ringing in the distance but didn't make a move to answer it. She didn't want to talk to anyone. She just wanted to be alone.

When she heard her front door open and then close, she knew her friends had gotten sick of waiting for her to answer her phone. But, it wasn't Leah or Mel who kneeled in front of her, it was Anthony.

"Hey." He brushed her hair from her face.

"What are you doing here?" she cried out.

"Leah and Melanie called me because they were worried about you and you weren't answering your phone."

"I'm fine." She averted her eyes from his. She didn't want to see him and have more emotions to deal with. "You should go."

"I know Reed leaving is difficult for you, but you have to let me in. Let everyone in. You don't have to do this alone."

"Yes, I do!" She sat up, pulling her knees to her chest. "You don't know what it feels like to love someone and then have that person ripped away from you!"

When silence settled in around her, she looked up to see Anthony staring at her slack-jawed. "You know, your stubbornness is one of the things I love about you, but right now," he shook his head, "you just have no idea."

He stood up. "When you decide you are ready to lean on someone, call me." He walked away, leaving her once again watching someone she loved walk away.

What was his problem? Why couldn't he understand how much pain she was in? Her heart was breaking and he didn't seem to care.

Not to mention, if he was the kind of person who would just walk away when she was hurting, maybe he wasn't the right person for her.

None of it made sense though. He'd held her hand through telling her dad, and been there to make sure she was okay when she told

Logan and Brandon. And, when she needed help with Reed, he had no problem stepping up to help.

Why was he being such a dick now?

It wasn't his style. She'd never seen him be anything but helpful.

Shaking her head in confusion, she stood. She had no idea what she wanted or needed to do, but she knew she couldn't sit around and wallow all day. Deciding cleaning up the house was a good place to start, she began picking up. She started in the living room, then went to the kitchen and bathrooms. The last place she went was Reed's room. As soon as she entered the room and saw all the toys, she broke down again. It was too much and she had no way to control her emotions. Each toy she picked up would remind her of a memory of Reed.

Picking up a stuffed dog, she hugged it to her chest and sat down on his bed. She was on the verge of a total meltdown when she heard Leah call her name from downstairs.

"Carly, are you here?"

Quickly wiping her eyes, she sat the stuffed dog down and stood up. There was no way her friend wouldn't be able to tell she'd been crying but there was nothing she could do about it.

Walking down the stairs, she found not only Leah but also Melanie. "Hey guys."

"Why the fuck weren't you answering your phone?" Mel said angrily. "We knew this was going to be hard and we wanted to help."

"I'm fine."

"Liar," Leah said. "Your eyes tell a different story."

"So I've been crying. People do it all the time."

"Yeah, but not you," Mel pointed out. "Talk to us."

"I don't want to talk about it." She walked past them and into her kitchen. "Reed is gone, and there is nothing I can do about it. Does it matter that I didn't want him to leave? That I fell in love with him? No, it doesn't. And to top it all off, I think Anthony hates me and now I have no one." She slammed her hand down on the counter in anger.

"First," Leah said, moving closer to her, "you don't have no one, you have us."

"Tell us what happened with Tony?" Mel was standing on the other side of the counter.

"I don't know. He came by and found me curled in a ball on the couch. I was angry and said something about him not knowing what it was like to fall in love with someone and then have them leave. He got pissed and left."

Melanie dropped her head backward and groaned. "Of course he was pissed. You insinuated that he had no idea how you were feeling when he is feeling the exact same way."

"What? How could he be feeling the same way? He didn't lose Reed."

"Didn't he?" Leah asked. "He spent a lot of time with him. Reed loved him and asked about him all the time. Whenever Tony was around, Reed wanted to be where he was. He spent virtually as much time with him as you did."

For a second the world stopped spinning. Carly didn't have words and couldn't think of any. Leah was right. How had she not seen that? Not recognizing that Reed had burrowed into a corner of Anthony's heart the same as he had hers? How had she been so blind?

When the world began moving again, panic of what she'd done bubbled to the surface. "Oh God, I pushed him away."

"Breathe," Mel said. "This is not unfixable."

"But what if it is? I can't lose him. I love him so much. He's everything. He makes me calm, and makes me think, and he loves me. No one's ever loved me like he has."

"So we need a plan," Leah said.

"A good one," Mel added.

"No," Carly said adamantly. "No plans. I have to fix this by groveling for forgiveness. I fucked up and I have to own it."

She knew that was the only way. He'd put his faith in her and she'd gone and stomped on it, all because she'd been heartbroken.

He deserved honesty and that's what she was going to give him.

Chapter 20

Tony left Carly's house like a bat out of hell. But when he got about two miles from her house, he pulled over. He was too worked up to drive and knew it was dangerous. How dare Carly pretend to know how he was or wasn't feeling. He slammed his hands against the steering wheel in rage. Did she really think he wasn't upset about Reed leaving?

He loved that little boy.

He sucked in a deep breath. Oh God, Reed was gone. Tears pooled in his eyes and he swiftly wiped them away. He wasn't one of those men who thought crying was only for women, but he also wasn't one who did it very often. He couldn't even remember the last time he'd cried.

It didn't matter though. Having Reed in his life for the last month had been pure joy, and now that he was gone, he had no problem showing emotion about it.

He just wished Carly understood how much he cared.

Starting the truck, he pulled back out onto the road and headed for home. Only he didn't want to go home and be alone. He was angry at Carly for shutting him out, but he still loved her and wanted to be with her. Turning his truck around, he headed into town. He'd get some coffee, maybe some food and hopefully after that, he'd have a plan.

He knew one thing for sure. He was not willing to let Carly push him away no matter how hard she tried.

Pulling into the diner in the center of town, he shut off the truck and got out. Inside, he looked for an empty table and spotted Brandon at a table in the back. Brandon noticed him too and waved him over.

"I don't normally see you here," Brandon said when he sat down. "Plus, I thought you'd be with Carly today?"

"She didn't want me there when she said goodbye." It still stung to remember her saying it and, when she'd first told him, he'd had to work hard not to react. He understood her reasoning but the fact that she didn't get that he was also losing Reed, pissed him off.

"I can tell from the look on your face you aren't happy about that."

"It's fine." He waved it off. "I'm more pissed off about what just happened."

"Oh hell, what did she do now?"

"I knew this was going to be a hard day for her, so I stopped by and found her curled in a ball on her couch." The image would haunt him forever. Tear stained cheeks, eyes red and blotchy. She'd been more than sad. She was heartbroken.

"Fuck!" he swore. "What have I done?" She'd been heartbroken and he'd been thinking only about himself.

"Something stupid, if I had to guess."

Tony let out an exasperated sigh. "You don't know the half of it."

"We all do stupid stuff. We're men; it's in our DNA." He took a sip of his coffee. "Now tell me what you did and I'll talk you through it."

"I got mad at her because she didn't seem to know she wasn't the only one who loved Reed. And I walked away. She was crying and heartbroken, and I walked away. What kind of person does that?"

"The kind who is in love and isn't making rational decisions. She'll forgive you."

"What if I never forgive myself?" He dropped his head into his hands. "You should have seen her face, Bran."

"I love Carly like a sister but she has a tendency to not look before she leaps. The one thing I do know about her is that she loves with her whole heart. And once she loves you, there is no getting rid of her. Believe me, I've tried."

Tony wanted to laugh at his joke but he was too torn up inside to find anything funny. "Tell me what I should do?"

"My advice, you go back over there and demand she forgives you."

He rolled his eyes. "Do you even know her? You can't demand anything from her. She'd squash me like a bug."

Brandon laughed. "Possibly. But if you love her – and I know you do – then you'd also know that she sometimes needs to be told what the right thing is. She gets caught up in her mind and tends to forget."

"And what's the right thing here?"

"That you weren't trying to hurt her. Make her understand you really do get what she is going through."

Brandon had a good point. He needed her to see he wasn't trying to undermine her emotions but show her that he felt the same way.

"I think you might be right."

"I'm always right. Just don't tell Leah."

Tony laughed, finally feeling a little lighter. He wouldn't be whole again until he talked to Carly, but he had hope they'd work it out.

After breakfast, he drove back to Carly's. There was no way he could wait any longer to talk to her. It was now or never. He practically ran to the door, knocking loudly. He waited a few seconds and when she didn't answer, he let himself in.

Max was lying on the couch and lifted his head when he heard Tony, but then set it back down immediately.

"Carly!" he shouted when he didn't spot her in the living room or kitchen. There was no answer, so he ran up the stairs to check her room. She wasn't there either, or in Reed's room or the bathroom.

Where could she be?

Back downstairs, he looked out the front door and, it was then, he noticed her car was gone. So she wasn't home, but where'd she go?

Pulling out his phone, he texted Melanie to see if she might know.

Tony:

Do you know where Carly is?

Melanie:

Maybe. Why?

Tony:

I'm at her house and she's not here. I really need to talk to her.
Melanie:
You're at her house?
Tony:
Yeah.
Melanie:
Stay there and don't go anywhere.
Tony:
I can't. I need to find Carly.
Melanie:
Trust me. Just. Stay. There.

Tony was confused and annoyed. He didn't want to stay there. He wanted to find Carly and tell her all the reasons why she shouldn't give up on him. But Mel knew Carly better than anyone, so, if she wanted him to stay, he would stay.

Taking a seat next to Max, he began petting the dog and going over everything he wanted to say. He didn't know how much time had passed but, abruptly, Carly finally came flying through the front door.

"Anthony," she said, her breathing heavy as if she'd just run a long distance.

He stood. "Carly, I'm so sorry I left earlier."

"No, I'm sorry. It never occurred to me that you were hurting too."

"I was...am, but I –" She cut him off.

"There are no buts." She took two steps toward him. "I was only thinking about myself and how I felt. Not once did I think about you and what you were going through. I'm the worst kind of person and saying I'm sorry will never be enough."

"It is enough," he said and stepped even closer to her. "I had all these things I wanted to apologize for, but none of them matter now. I don't want you to feel bad for being sad and missing Reed. I just want to offer comfort and support. To be here for you, no matter what." He was close enough to touch her then, and he did. Stroking a hand down her face he said, "I love you, Carly, so much that when you hurt, I hurt. And seeing you torn up over the loss of Reed, that was the worst kind of torture."

She gripped his hand and held it against her face. "I was sad but when you left, it was worse. So much worse. I thought I was losing you too, and as heartbroken as I was with Reed leaving," she shook her head, "I wanted to vomit. I was, literally, sick to my stomach."

"You're not losing me. Ever." Finally he kissed her. She was as urgent as he was as their lips and tongues collided. She was gripping the front of his shirt in her fists, and he cupped her head in his hands, as they told each other without words, how much they loved one another.

They were both breathing heavily when she pulled away. "You told me once that I had to choose the life I wanted." She searched his face. "I choose you. And I won't settle for anything less than all of you. The good parts where you love me, laugh with me and take care of me. The bad parts where you leave your clothes on the floor, eat like a ten-year-old and annoy me, and the ugly parts where you leave me crying on the couch. I want them all."

He leaned his forehead against hers. "The first two I can give you, but if it's okay with you, I'd rather never see you crying on the couch again."

"No promises." She smiled up at him. "I love you. So much."

"I love you too." He kissed her lightly. "Tell me about your night with Reed?"

She sighed. "He was upset and angry and he didn't want to go. Ryan took it hard and left for a few hours."

"Where'd he go?"

"I have no idea but, he was here this morning when I woke up." She took his hand in hers and walked with him to the couch, where they sat. "He's unhappy. I can tell he wants to make a change but he doesn't know how. I'm hoping Reed will have a positive effect on him."

"I don't see how he can't. That kid is a joy to be around."

Her face fell. "How are we going to go from being with him every day to only seeing him monthly or hell, maybe not even that?"

"I don't know," he said. "But we'll figure it out together."

"Together," she repeated his words, looking down at their joined hands. "I like the sound of that."

They spent the rest of the weekend together, supporting and comforting each other. Being with her was so easy that sometimes Tony felt like it wasn't real. But then, he would touch her or kiss her, or even make love to her, and he knew she was as real as could be.

When Monday came, they both had work, and that meant hours apart. Hours he spent at Logan's gallery, trying to finish up the security system. He was just about finished when his phone rang. Seeing it was Carly, he picked up.

"Hey, beautiful."

"Anthony, you have to come over right now."

Immediately, he dropped his drill on the counter and headed out to his truck. "Is everything okay? What's wrong?" Only she didn't sound panicked. She sounded...happy.

"Just come." The line went dead. He stared at his phone in disbelief. She'd hung up on him. Shaking his head to clear away the confusion, he put his truck in gear and hightailed it to her house. When he pulled up, he saw not just her car, but also another one. Wondering who could be there, he strode toward the front door when, all of a sudden, it flew open and Reed came running out, leaping into his arms.

"We came back!" he yelled, as Tony enveloped him in his arms. "We came back," he said again, only quieter.

"I see that," Tony said in shock. He looked up and saw Carly – a smile bigger than the sun on her face – watching from the deck. Ryan was standing next to her, also smiling.

When Max nudged his nose between Reed and him, Reed laughed and began petting him.

Standing, Tony looked from the boy and dog to Carly and Ryan. "What's going on?"

"Reed and I talked when we were in Baltimore and we both decided we liked it better in Cedarville."

"We're moving here," Reed said from the ground.

"What about your job?"

"He quit," Carly spoke for him.

"I was miserable in that job," Ryan said. "I decided I want more."

Carly's eyes were shining bright with love as she watched him. Tony saw Ryan walk away as he moved up the stairs, eventually standing right in front of her.

"It seems like you're about to get everything you wanted."

She bit her bottom lip. "More like everything I never knew I wanted, but actually did want."

He laughed. "It must be true love if I understood what you just said."

"Do you have a problem with that?"

He looked back at Reed, then back to her. Taking her in his arms, he lifted her off her feet and spun her around. "Hell no."

Also by Bree Kraemer
The Only Series
Only By His Touch
Only With Trust
If Only
Only You
Only For Love
Cedarville Series
An Unexpected Home
Capturing Us
Choosing You
Better Together
A Chance Worth Taking
Forever Starts Here (Novella)
After All These Years
Won't Let You Down
Say When
Something to Lose
Finally Home
Friends & Brothers
Sky High Love
Bridge To Love
When It's Love
Rockstar Romance
The Right Note
Pick Me
Christmas Novella
Light Me Up
DecorHate for the Holidays
Falling Over You
The Beckmeyer Family
Hooked

Sparked
Shocked
Kneaded
Valley Falls Strikers
Late Tackle
First Touch
Give & Go
Narrowing the Angle
He's A Keeper
Ground Rule
Walk Off
Sacrifice Bunt
Grand Slam (coming soon)